A. S .O. D

A. S. O. D.

A Series of Dreams

Troy Kindred

BRAMBLEWOOD PRESS, LLC
SANTA BARBARA, CALIFORNIA

ISBN: 978-0-9797665-3-4

Published by
Bramblewood Press, LLC
729 De La Vina Street
Santa Barbara, CA 93101

Printed in the United States of America

*To the pessimistic optimists who strive to elevate
the human condition despite the obvious
shortcomings of this world.*

Contents

ZAHAVA

D ad, the homeless lady is standing by our car."
"It's all right, Mary. All she wants is some change."
"Won't she just go away?"
"Honey she's been in this town for as long as I can remember. One thing I can say is, we do take care of our homeless. At least we feed them…or, at least, somebody does. Here, you push the cart and I'll carry the water."

A man and his teenage daughter, average in every way, make their way out of the hometown grocery store only to be confronted by the local transient.

"Dad, can we just go back and shop some more until she leaves?"

"No Baby, we can't. Now come on."

"Please?"

"I said, 'no!' Now come on! Your mom's waiting for us."

The transient was a grossly obese woman with scraggly long matted gray hair. Her skin was dark and rugged from years of direct exposure to the harsh rays of the sun, a byproduct, one of many, of homelessness.

Deeply soiled, mix-matched clothing covered most of her body. She wasn't a tall woman, no more then five feet two. But, bad posture made her appear much shorter.

Just as they returned to their vehicle, a late model white Volvo, the woman began mumbling to herself, then dropped down out of view along the passenger side of the car.

"Hang on," the father said, stopping his daughter from getting any closer. He cautiously walked around to the side where the woman had disappeared, only to find her on her hands and knees trying to look under the vehicle. He came close enough to discern…or at least he thought he could discern…what she was saying. As he expected, it made no sense to him.

From his vantage point, her body looked like a large pile of dirty rags someone had discarded between parking spaces. Her hair almost perfectly blended with the discolored oily asphalt. She strained to get a better look under the car.

"Is that you?" she said, with an old raspy voice. She wasn't concerned with the man standing just a few feet away. "I need you. Please, come back to me."

The father had heard enough and decided to put an end to the nonsense and get his daughter and himself home. He walked up to the woman who was still looking under the car. "I'm sorry, lady, but…"

He was cut short by the meowing of a cat coming from under the car.

"Dad, it's a cat!" said his daughter, excitedly. "Can we keep it?"

"No, honey. It's probably her cat."

"Dad, we have a place for it to stay. She doesn't."

"Mary," the father said sternly, "that was not called for."

"I miss you so much," the women said, drawing the father's attention back to the problem: getting the lady and her cat away from the car so they could leave.

The father looked around the lot for store security but saw no one. It appeared that he and his daughter were on their own.

He spoke to the women in a calm reassuring voice, "Ma'am, if you just move back, I'll help you get your cat."

The woman turned and looked directly at him.

He gazed into the depths of her green eyes and, at that moment, experienced something strange. They were so demanding, but at the same time gentle.

He tried to take a step back but couldn't. The sound of his daughter's voice pulled him from the hypnotic tug of war he had found himself in.

"Dad, what are you doing?"

He backed away and half spun to face his daughter. "Honey, lets go."

"But, dad, what about the cat and the…"

He put more strength into his voice. "They'll move. Now get in the car!"

"The groceries…"

"Now! I'll worry about the groceries."

His daughter complied, leaving him standing there, facing the direction were his daughter once stood. The entire time the silhouette of the transient woman impressed itself on his periphery. He slowly turned back toward her, avoiding eye contact.

She hadn't moved. Even without looking directly into her eyes, he knew she was probing, sizing him up.

"I'm sorry," he told her. "We won't be able to help you, lady. We're very late." He hurried to the cart of groceries.

The woman watched his every move.

Pulling the cart to the rear he popped the trunk and quickly unloaded their purchases.

"Is it you?" the woman said.

He knew she was speaking to him but did not answer. Moving faster, he threw the last bag into the trunk, spilling most of its contents. Keys in hand, he slammed down the lid of the trunk and hurried to the driver's door, an escape portal out of the bizarre nightmare he found himself in. He focused hard on the door as he moved toward it. Trying to make himself as thin as possible, he slid past the woman, who grabbed at him the moment he came between her and the car.

Within seconds he was in his seat, door shut and locked, keys in the ignition.

"What a freak," said the daughter looking out her window. "Dad, the cat just ran away. Run kitty, the crazy lady might eat you."

"Honey, please." He started the car, put it into reverse and slowly backed out, checking that the old lady wasn't in the way. As he made the final turn of the wheel, something inside made him briefly look back.

It was just long enough to see damp streams running down from eyes full of tears. How could a human being reach such a low point, he thought.

Driving off, he fought the urge to look back again.

Zahava stood there and watched the white station wagon diminish as it moved farther and farther away.

"I am Zahava…I am Zahava," she mumbled, running the thought through her mind over and over again. But each new moment brought a rush of voices and images that tipped her mental scale further toward insanity. She knew it would not be long before her thoughts would be overcome by this alternate reality - a reality full of falsehood and corruption. She made her way to a nearby park.

"I am Zahava."

Like a lone fighter surrounded by a relentless enemy she stood her ground in that vast cerebral terrain called the mind.

"I am Zahava. I am Zahava."

The voices of children crying rose up around her. She looked about frantically but saw nothing.

"I am Zahava."

Flickering images of human beings in various states of death and dying leaped forward, assaulting what little sanity she had left.

"I am Zahava."

She sat down on the first bench she could find. At that moment a cold chill came over her and she knew that the final attack was beginning. She lowered her head, relaxed and slowed her breathing.

"I am Zahava. I must…sleep…to wake up."

The perception of her surroundings narrowed, then diminished.

"Zahava! Wake up!"

Zahava, a radiant human creature, sat on a chair formed of rock. From her flawless skin to her long golden hair every part of her body gave off a soft glow.

"Zahava, are you back with us?"

She lifted her head slowly, and glanced around the room. Her clear green eyes perceived three males and another female standing around a large stone slab. A fourth male lying on his back, eyes closed, arms folded across his chest.

They wore robes that were anthracite in color and glittered when they moved.

"Zahava, are you all right?"

Zahava's chair was positioned at the head of the male who was lying on the slab. "I know I was close," she said, staring down at the body. "He was there somewhere."

One of the men standing around the table spoke. "We've lost five gods in the last two thousand years with only one human and one insectan ascending to our level in more then four thousand. Will there be a time when gods are no more than a thing of the past?"

"To mortals," replied Zahava, "There will always be gods." With only a thought she shifted the room's magnetic field creating a tingling sensation on the skin of the occupants. "The all powerful watchers." Her voice raised then echoed throughout the room. "Immortal and benevolent, giving them hope."

The same male who spoke earlier responded by levitating his body off the ground and putting equal force behind his words. "Look!" he said, pointing at the body. "Are we not mortal?" He descended, his voice lowered. "The creatures you call 'mortal' only believe we live forever because their lives are only a fraction of ours." His voice rose again. "Nothing, Zahava, lasts forever. To solidify that fact," he gestured again toward the body, "you are about to lose your loved one." The words reminded all in the room why they where there: To give comfort to one of their own in his passing.

"Zahava, you have a choice." The male speaker dematerialized and re-appeared beside her. He gently placed a hand on her shoulder. "You can let him slip away in a confused, illogical fantasy, or you can risk re-entering his subconscious and try to make his final dream a lucid one."

The determination that showed on her face, answered his question. She turned her attention to the body. The male next to her asked one last question. "What is he dreaming?"

"A world of vanity and decay," she replied. "I believe his mind's name for it was 'Earth.'"

"He's falling into the darker regions of his consciousness. You must hurry!"

Quickly, she lowered her head and let her thoughts spiral into her own subconscious, that place that all in the room knew to be a higher realm of thought.

Spinning upwards, she moved through the dream state, passing by memories of past events, strung together in mix-matched patches of varying lengths of time.

Up…and up…and up, finally emerging like an amphibian from a pond only to find itself surrounded by an ocean for as far as the eye could see.

All who had ascended to this state recognized this place and knew that nothing compared to its vastness…where the inner minds of every sentient being connected, drawing energy from one another, the negative and the positive.

Zahava focused her thoughts on the one she sought and in an instant was confronted with the mind of her loved one.

Its external energy was chaotic, but she knew what to do: match its vibrations, then find the area responsible for his basic senses, then bind with them. His mind would interpret this new entry into its dream in its own way…in her case, a homeless woman.

Once inside, she had no time to waste. The longer she remained there, the more her own thoughts would mesh with his imaginary world. It wasn't a matter of scouring an entire dream landscape, for in someone else's dream it made no difference where you were, they were there, too. Somewhere. She just had to find where his mind was centered, be it an inanimate object or a creature, like a dog or a cat, then coax him out of the state of lower energy, pseudo logic into the higher energy logic of truth…that is if he still possessed enough energy to make the change.

Almost…almost…

"You old lady. Get off our lawn!"

Zahava was standing in what she reasoned was the front lawn of the home of the father and daughter she had encountered earlier. The young girl stood at the doorway of the house with an annoyed expression on her face.

"Dad," the girl said, speaking loudly. "I think she slept here last night." She waved a hand in front of her face. "And she stinks."

"Honey," The father's voice could be heard from inside, "why don't you invite her in?"

"What?"

"Hurry up and shut the door."

The girl stepped to one side and held the door for Zahava to enter.

Zahava approached the house cautiously. Something about the girl's willingness to accede to her father's demand wasn't consistent with the last encounter.

Could this be it, she thought to herself. Even the rudimentary logic energy that sustains this world was breaking down. If a complete loss of energy were to happen, his death, were to happen while she was inside, it could take a part of her mind with it.

When gods succumb to fear, she thought, then, all hope is lost. She walked inside.

Once there, she saw the father sitting at a dining room table, which confirmed the worst. What little energy he had left was being used to sustain the arena she had now found herself in. A dining room…the last bit of a dissipating illusion in the mind of a dying god.

The room was small and sparsely furnished. A series of six light sources, glass bulbs shaped like tear drops, lined the walls. One of the bulb's luminance wavered in and out.

"Have a seat," the father said. He glanced at a chair next to the table then back at Zahava.

Too late, she thought, I'm too late…I should leave now.

"Please stay," the father said, now smiling.

She complied.

"My daughter really doesn't like you," he said, looking directly into her eyes.

For some reason she had trouble recognizing their color. "You know," she replied, "most mortals are afraid of the unknown, so that void is sometimes filled with falsehood to compensate for their lack of understanding."

"Yes…yes, I think you're right." The father's expression became neutral.

"Your daughter was snared by my outward appearance."

The waning bulb went out. Two more began to dim. Zahava took note.

"Hey," the father said, "my daughter isn't the brightest star in the sky but you don't have to put her down."

"I wasn't…"

"You are in my house and you will show my daughter and me some respect!"

"I am in his house, she thought…another anomaly…he invited me in."

The two dimming bulbs blinked out.

"My time is up."

"I think you should leave." The father stood and pointed toward a door at the rear of the room that Zahava didn't remember being there. She glanced back where she had entered and saw only a wall.

Two more of the remaining lights flickered, and then, were no more. The room was instantly awash in twilight. She had to take that exit. She knew the dream would collapse at any moment. This was all that was left of the deteriorating aspiration his subconscious called Earth: a dining room with an angry father figure pointing her toward a mysterious door.

Sadness engulfed her.

She made her way to the exit, grabbed the knob, but stopped just short of opening it. She turned to get one last look at a dying god's swan song… Earth…so sad.

The entire room seemed to blink repeatedly into darkness and back. She faced the door, gripped the knob tightly and turned. Suddenly it flung open.

Like a tidal wave engulfing a small island, her movements were puppet-like as she made her way deeper into the brightness. The same force that was compelling her toward it caused her to stop.

Like a container being drained of water, the scene of pure light lowered and fell away, leaving behind a crisp blue sky and gentle rolling hills filled with multicolored beds of flowers as far as her eye could see. Butterflies of various colors, shapes and sizes danced from petal to petal, alighting momentarily before twirling off into the air, looping their paths with others.

Her thoughts halted. She didn't know how to interpret what she was experiencing. But, before she had a chance to consider the possibilities, a loud booming male voice could be heard throughout the land.

"Now," said the voice. "This is what Earth should have been. All of its creatures joined together in harmony under their god."

Zahava smiled. A path opened up before her. In the distance a man appeared standing straight and strong. The same man she had left dying on a table just moments earlier.

With outstretched arms he motioned to the fields around them. "Zahava," his voice lowered. "Do you like it?"

She struggled for words.

"I know how much you like flowers."

"You…you're lucid."

"Yes, I am."

"But this place. How much energy are you using…?"

"Enough. If I'm going to die why not end it giving something to someone I care for?"

"But that other place…I thought…"

"You mean the Earth dream."

She nodded.

"That world my mind had created was so insidious that it was too difficult and exhaustive for me to dissolve. So I separated myself from it."

"I see."

"We all have our dark side."

"I know," said Zahava. "And I understand. I saw glimpses of that world. There were so many aspects of you. So many…gods…so fragmented."

"I am sorry."

"Don't be."

A sudden drop in temperature rekindled Zahava's sense of urgency. "You're losing energy."

"I know."

"We have to do something."

"It's too late."

She looked at the land around her. "You must save your energy. This place is unnecessary."

"It's for you."

Zahava's voice sounded with force. "I demand that you end this!"

"I cannot."

"Yes, you can. You must use this energy to take control of your body."

"It's not enough."

"It has to be enough. Gods should not die!"

A whirlwind quickly appeared off to her left, highlighted by a strand of butterflies lacing the spiral stream of air. The wind shifted to where she stood, incasing her in a soft funnel of colors.

"Zahava," he said in a calm gentle voice, "I didn't want the other dream to be my final one. I am dying. That cannot be changed. Beings that strive toward immortality are nothing more then delusional lingerers, grasping onto something that can never be. If you truly care about me, accept this gift around you and remember what I was and what I meant to you for as long as you can."

She felt the temperature drop again. The forcefulness in her voice was replaced by urgency. "I cannot let you go."

"Yes, you can."

This time the temperature dropped drastically. The outskirts of the horizon became hazy.

"Please, no." She could see her breath. Tears raced down from the corners of her eyes. "You were a mighty god."

"I am about to become one with the mightiest god of all, the Infinite."

The haze moved in, leaving her standing on what looked like a tiny life raft covered with flowers.

"Good-bye, Zahava."

His image faded. All that was left was a patch of land just large enough to lodge her feet.

When she lowered her head to depart, a delicate pulse of air touched her lips…a good-bye kiss.

She found herself back in the room where she had started, head bowed in deep contemplative thought. The now deceased body of a fellow god lay in front of her. The voice of one of the others present pulled her from a cocoon of self-reflection.

"Zahava, what did you learn?"

She stood, staring off into the distance. "He is dead."

In a flash she disappeared, leaving her astral image behind and her final words.

"I've learned how little I do know."

Then, it too was gone.

Evil, Cha Ching

Inside a local bar two middle-aged women sat by the door. One of them was tall with long black hair, green eyes and an athletic build, and the other average in height, short red hair and brown eyes. They both wore little jewelry and light make-up.

Late evening. A yellow sun began to disappear behind a row of businesses across the street. Its rays reached in through the large open doors of the bar, illuminating two half full margaritas sitting in front them. They faced each other, talking.

"So what club are we hitting tonight?" Asked the black haired woman to her partner.

"I don't know, but if you have another margarita, we're not going anywhere."

"I've only had one more than you."

"The hell you have, bitch."

"The hell I have, skank."

"I don't think so, slut."

"I think so, pendeja"

They both started to giggle when a tall, well built man in slacks and dress shirt walked through the door of the bar. He appeared to be of European descent and carried himself very well. He sat down in a corner booth, glanced over at them, smiled, and then turned his attention to a waitress who walked up to take his order.

One of the women turned to the other. "He's mine."

"I saw him first."

"You're too short."

"Really? Well, I think men want a woman who looks up to them."

"Ya know he looks Swedish, and I'm part Swedish."

"I think he looks English."

The waitress moved away from his table. He pulled out a small pad and paper and began making notations on it. His facial expression was neutral except for a soft gentle smile on his lips.

"He must be rich," said the black-haired woman.

"Think so?"

"I can tell."

"How?"

"Look at him. I mean look at his face. He's so content."

"Yeah, and…"

"No worries."

Just then the same waitress stood beside them. "What would you like to drink?"

"We're OK," said the short-haired woman.

"It's OK," replied the waitress. "It's paid for."

They looked at each other, then at the man in the booth, still making notes on his pad.

"Paid for?" one of them asked the waitress.

"Yes, by that man over there." She pointed at the gentleman they had been eying.

Again they looked at each other, and smiled. At the same time they gestured toward the half empty drinks in front of them.

"Margaritas?" asked the waitress in confirmation.

They nodded with playful enthusiasm.

The waitress took their order and walked away.

"OK," said the woman with black hair. "Which one of us is gonna get up, walk over there and thank him?"

"Shouldn't we wait for him to come over here?" said the other woman.

"Maybe you're right."

One of them took a sip of her drink, followed by the other.

A minute or two went by with them trying not to look over at the man before the waitress returned.

"I've had enough," said the black haired woman.

"And?"

"I'm going over there."

"To give him my number?" said the other. "Thanks. I'll write it down for you."

Her friend laughed. "Bitch," then stood and started toward the man. About halfway there, a blond female equal in height abruptly cut her off. Her tanned athletic body pushed past her to where the man was sitting. The blonder was wearing tight, formfitting clothing that emphasized her over-developed breast, and high heels. Bright red lipstick punctuated her large lips. She scooted in next to him.

Surprised and embarrassed, the black-haired woman made her way back to her girlfriend and her margarita.

"Womanizer!" said her redheaded friend as the other woman sat down.

"I almost made a complete fool of myself," the black-haired woman said.

"Think of it like this," replied her partner. "At least we got free drinks out of the bastard."

They high fived each other, almost missing hands.

"I think we've had enough to drink," said one of them.

"Right," replied the other.

They couldn't help but notice the blonder who had joined the man shake her head, 'no,' periodically.

"Let's sit here for a minute and cool down before we leave," said the woman with black hair. "One of us has to drive."

"Good idea."

The combination of little action taking place around the bar and the alcohol they consumed was mesmerizing. Their gazes seesawed back and forth from the booth where the couple was sitting to their drinks.

Across the room, the motion of the man and blonder standing to leave broke their trance.

"You ready to go?" asked the black-haired woman.

"Yeah, I'm ready."

The man and woman had now made their way close to where the ladies were sitting. The man stopped with his back to them. He was inches away from the woman with black hair. Even then it was hard for the two women to understand what they were saying but they could see the blonder girl respond to the man by shaking her head, "no," again. As he was talking, the man reached one hand into his pocket, pulled it out and held it closed behind his back.

They had planned to leave but curiosity held the two women firmly in their seats.

The man gestured with the closed hand behind his back, as if to get the attention of the two women behind him. They both focused on the closed hand.

It opened.

Lying neatly in its palm was a crisp once-folded thousand dollar bill. The black-haired woman looked at her friend. She pointed at herself and mouthed, "For me?"

Her friend, shaking her head yes, mouthed back, "take it".

The thought of making money and being a part of something… naughty…intrigued them both. The black-haired woman reached over and plucked the money out of his hand. Before she could withdraw her arm the man turned and faced them.

"I'd like to introduce you to my sister and her best friend. She's out visiting." His voice was supple and sweet. And when he smiled his clear blue eyes sparkled.

There was a pause.

"Introduce yourselves. Please."

Then a brief hesitation. "I…uhm. Uhm…I'm Mary and this is my friend, Carol."

"Your brother is so nice," said the blonder, "He invited me over to his place for a movie and drinks tonight."

"Really," said the black-haired woman smiling.

"I was hesitant at first, since we just met yesterday. But seeing how close he is to his family and he did introduce me to you…well…what could it hurt?" She looked at the man. "K, I'll be there."

"Great," answered the man. "I'll see you then." He gently kissed her on the cheek. "Let me walk you out."

"Alright," said the blonder They exited together.

The two women looked at each other with big eyes. "Can you believe that shit?" said the red head. "I guess he's gonna score tonight."

"Yeah, and I told you he was rich," replied the other. She waved the thousand dollar bill in front of her.

Gesturing in unison, they made the old time cash sound. "Cha ching."

The short-haired woman looked over at the table where the man was sitting. "Hey, he left something."

The other one stood to see. "It's the pad he was writing on." Still holding the money, she hurried over, picked it up, and was out the door after him.

Outside she saw a black limousine down the street. He was just getting in. "Hey, wait you forgot something!" She started running toward him. He didn't seem to hear. "Hey!" she yelled. She made it to the vehicle just as he shut the door. His window was down.

"Your pad!" She signaled with the bill. "I hope she was worth it," she said, catching her breath.

He smiled and took it from her.

"Don't thank us for getting you laid tonight," she said.

He looked down at the hand that was holding the money. His smile became grotesquely large. "You have no idea the amount of pleasure I'm going to have."

He looked up into her eyes and at that moment the man's physical beauty and something purely evil, became one.

He tapped the pad on the windowsill of the limo. "And I thought she wasn't going to make the list."

"List?" she murmured.

His next words sent a stinging chill through her entire body.

"I'm going to liquidate this one slowly." The limo started, then pulled away.

Stunned, she watched as it disappeared from view.

The promissory note slipped from her trembling fingers and fell onto the cold lifeless sidewalk.

Bob Johnson

* * * * * * I * * * * * *

Gaseous water molecules ascend toward the heavens, suddenly releasing the heat energy that gave birth to their rise. Falling back to the earth in the form of rain, they leave behind the energy that spawned their existence. That energy, once again, forces it's way back into the eternal cycle of nature in the form of lightning, searching the earth below for that return portal, that conduit back to the processes from which it came.

Like a seasoned cowboy dismounting his steed, Bob Johnson flung himself off his trusty John Deere tractor. His muscular middle-aged frame twisted naturally, landing next to his loyal workhorse.

Noticing the gathering storm clouds in the distance, his brown eyes swept mechanically, surveying the crops laid out before him. Wisps of cool Kansas air tempered the perspiration on his scalp through his close-cropped black hair, rewarding his day's work. Loose fitting overalls covered most of his body. An old T-shirt with sweat stains at the pits and worn dark brown work boots covered the rest, depriving all but his face and head of the refreshing night air.

A series of numbers ran through his mind. Times, dates, deadlines and commitments. The ex- wife's demands the night before. Maybe a new lawyer would be required. Maybe a new…

Like a flip of a light switch, all thoughts were replaced by complete vacuous darkness.

Flashes of light interposed with synchronous hurried voices penetrated his awareness; the distinct pressure of hands pushing and pulling, adjustments being made, the feeling of urgency.

More voices

One of our leads is off the monitor.

Get another line going wide open.

Call lab, we're going to need a CBC, chem-twelve, CKMB and Troponin.

Has anybody paged respiratory?

Time and pain are super induced, twisting and turning in an endless dance, pain relentlessly drawing time close to it, controlling it, slowing its pace.

He's having arrhythmias!

Doc, we've got irregular tachycardia with PVC's over here.

There he goes!

I think he's in v-fib.

…Shock him!

Ready………………..Clear

Ready………………..Clear

Ready………………..Clear

Three successive bursts of intense pain, followed by nothingness.

Like a butterfly unburdening itself from a cocoon, the feeling of his body slipping away is replaced by the sensation of weightlessness, ascension, the distinct images of people moving below, manipulating a half-draped body.

As an image on still waters disturbed, the view rippled and distorted. Suddenly flashes of familiar scenes emerged, each appearing then being replaced by new scenes. Childhood memories raced by, chaperoned by the feelings and emotions that corresponded to not only one, but all the participants in each reconnaissance.

The stream of experiences surged forward, slowing at the image of a man standing in a field. Farmland lay all around. Loose fitting overalls cover most of his body. An old T-shirt with sweat stains and worn dark brown work boots covered the rest.

The duality of seeing and experiencing filled his awareness. A replay of thoughts cut short by an intense energy from above, engulfed his body…an event so swift that emotion was inconceivable. The force that felt almost living instantly entered through his ears and mouth, rushing through his body, snapping out at his right foot. He fell face first next to an old tractor. Complete darkness.

All images ceased.

Then…

At the periphery of his perceptual awareness, he felt a distinct presence...something familiar. It was like a vague memory, but something he had known all of his life. It came closer, moving in from all sides, soothing his thoughts. An all-embracing feeling of caring and love suffused his being.

Instantly all focus changed. Darkness was slowly breached by an illumination in the distance, pulling him closer. The distinction either of him moving or it advancing or expanding in size was confused.

As if produced in his own mind, thoughts materialized. Questions were asked of him. "Are you ready? You're not? Return now or wait? Now..."

A rush of knowledge was imparted. A gift.

With a flash, a previous scene appeared. Below, three men and one woman encircled his body. All but one stepped away simultaneously. He slipped back in.

Ready...................Clear

I've got a rhythm and pulse.

It doesn't look like we're going to have to intubate.

He's breathing on his own.

Pupils are dilated but slightly reactive.

Blood pressure's ninety over sixty.

We need to push more fluids. Hang another bag of normal saline.

Time elapsed.

The sound of buzzing was accompanied by memories of growing up as a little girl in Missouri...two caring parents, old boy friends, the one that broke my heart, my little girl, my husband, my name...my name.

"My name is Susan Fischer." Bob Johnson responded fully to the question asked of him.

Glancing down at her badge then back at the patient, a tall slender redheaded nurse reiterated. "You're obviously oriented enough to read my name badge, but your name's not Susan. It's Robert Johnson. Let's try this again." She slid her stool closer. "Do you know where you are?"

Putting down the radiating pain from his right foot and the intense aching in his head, he focused on the question. Looking around, he slowly answered. "I've been hurt?"

"Good answer." She smiled thinly then continued. "Your neighbor stopped by your place and found you in the field unconscious. He called for help and our paramedics picked you up and brought you here."

Staring he asked. "How long was I...?" He broke off.

"We don't know," she said. "Maybe twenty…twenty-five minutes. You're a very lucky man. Most strike victims don't fair so well."

"Strike?"

"You were struck by lightening." she said, showing concern.

He slipped into silent reflection. Like a damaged ship looking for mooring, his mind searched for some mental anchor, some foundation of who he really was.

A name surfaced, escorted by a full life's memories. He spoke with profound relief. "I'm Robert Lewis Johnson."

Nurse Fischer stood, sliding her stool behind her. She said with assurance, "You're going to be OK, Mr. Johnson. Your neighbor gave us the name of your ex-wife. He thought she would be the one to notify. We found her number in your wallet, so we left a message but she hasn't called back yet." She put her hand on his shoulder. "Is there anyone else you would like us to contact?"

"No," he hesitated. "We never had kids; my closest relative is miles away." He tried to rise. "My neighbor can give me…" He lost his breath and fell back into bed.

"I don't think so," said Nurse Fischer with authority. "You're going to remain in the hospital for at least three days." She crossed her arms, then continued. "And from there, the doctor will decide if you're ready to be discharged. You've been lucky so far, so who knows." Her shoulders seemed to relax as her arms fell to her sides. "I'm off in about twenty minutes but my relief will see about getting you admitted, and answering any other questions you may have." She finished with a half wave. "Good-bye, Mr. Johnson, and good luck. Maybe I'll see you before you're discharged."

Staring with acceptance, he watched her slowly step back and turn away. The feeling of wanting to speak but not knowing what to say emerged. An opportunity lost.

She disappeared from view.

* * * * * * 11 * * * * * *

A row of accreditations lined the walls behind a large oak desk. A bookshelf stood at either side. More shelves to the front and rear, cluttered with items of various sizes, some recognizable, some not. Ethnic looking statuettes sat on the floor at all four corners, wooden busts of African origin towards the front with their Asian counterparts opposing them at opposite ends, an antechamber, turned office, to an exam room, a seemingly failed attempt at balance.

A large, balding grey-haired man removed an ashtray with his right hand while wiping fallen ashes to the floor with the other. He pulled a chart from his desk, glanced at a calendar on the wall and made a mental note. Five o'clock - golf -village clubhouse. His attention fell back to the chart, but before opening it, he checked the time on his desk clock. Four o'clock. Systematically he flipped through the pages, stopping periodically at certain items, skipping others. As his final summations began the intercom sounded.

There was a soft female voice. "Dr. Hendrickson?"

"Yes, Mary."

"There is a Robert L. Johnson here to see you."

"He's late! Send him in."

"Yes, Sir."

Seconds later two knocks are heard and a tall man appeared in the doorway. Loose fitting blue jeans and a white button-up shirt hid his physique. Clean black hiking boots added another half inch to his already six foot five inch frame.

He spoke as he looked over the office. "I'm sorry I'm late Doc, but my neighbor had to run some errands before he could pick me up."

Dr. Hendrickson gestured to a chair at the front of his desk, saying, "Come in, have a seat." He squared the chart he had been looking at in front of him.

With a limp yielding to his right side, Robert slowly made his way to a waiting chair.

"I'm a little short on time," said Dr. Hendrickson. "I'll try and make this as brief as possible." He glanced down at his desk clock then continued. "I've got more patients to see after five," he chuckled. "And I'm only one man." Flipping open the chart he said with confidence. "I've thoroughly gone over your records and don't see any reason why my associate's recommendations shouldn't be followed." He turned more pages and then stopped. "The medication he prescribed…let's see." He silently read a couple of lines then mumbled. "Three hundred milligrams Dilantin per day to be taken at night, and Xanax, one milligram three times a day." He looked up. "Doesn't seem to be working. Is that correct?"

"No." Robert answered. "No, not really."

"It's not correct?"

"I mean, 'no,' it doesn't seem to be working. I've had two seizures since I started on the stuff." Anxiety was in his voice. "And the things I see really worry me."

"Robert." Dr. Hendrickson shifted forward in his chair as if to rise but didn't. "What concerns me just as much are the results of your M.R.I. Dr. Baker and I both noticed an abnormality in your frontal lobe connection." He leaned to his right and rested his chin on his hand. "That could explain the strange things you've been seeing during seizure activity."

"But the things I see," Robert searched his mind for a way to explain. "They involve whoever is with me at the time." He paused. "I've tried not to mention it. I don't want people to think I'm nuts."

Dr. Hendrickson closed the chart then looked over at his clock. "Well, I wouldn't know anything about what you're seeing, but I can tell you this: It's not normal." He attempted to sit up straight but his large body slumped forward. "Neither Dr. Baker nor I have seen anything quite like this before. So, what I'm recommending is that you be seen by another neurologist. Someone with a subspecialty dealing with this type of disorder."

"I have to come back to Kansas City?" Robert asked, uncomfortably rocking forward in his chair. "I've got deadlines to meet." He shifted back. "The workers I hired need to be supervised." He paused. "Doc, I've got wife problems that…"

Dr. Hendrickson cut him off. "Now listen here, son." He spoke forcefully. "We've got to move this thing along!" His voice raised then lowered. "I mean, if you want to get better soon you've got to do what it takes." Clasping his hands together in prayer fashion, he leaned forward. "I had Mary, my secretary, search my files for any other neurologists specializing in this type of disorder."

"But Doc," Robert said in protest. "I don't think I can…"

Again, Dr. Hendrickson cut him off. "Robert, we all have our problems. If you want to get better, this is what you have got to do." He took a deep breath. "You need to make the necessary arrangements. Maybe a relative or your neighbor could watch your place for a couple of weeks until you return."

"A couple of weeks!" Robert tried to comprehend what to him was an enormous amount of time and at the same time absorb what he just heard. "Why a couple of weeks?"

"Unfortunately," said Dr. Hendrickson, "The doctor that Mary located practices at UCLA."

"You mean California?"

"Yes, Los Angeles."

Like an obese chef at a pretentious restaurant, Dr. Hendrickson served Robert his final meal of the day, seasoned with depression and anxiety, but lacking that one main ingredient - Time.

The magnitude of his condition started to sink in as Dr. Hendrickson's voice broke his trance. "My secretary will assist you in making any necessary arrangements." He started to stand. "Stop at her desk on the way out." He walked by Robert who was still seated, patted him on his shoulder and walked to the door. "Robert," he said reassuringly, "we're doing what we can."

Holding the door, Dr. Hendrickson waited for Robert to stand and start out. "Keep me informed." The door clicked shut behind him.

Outside the office, a thin-faced blonde secretary scanned him briefly and then returned her attention to a set of notes she had made. Her petite body was humped over as she read aloud.

An odd thought entered Robert's mind. What could have happened in this woman's life to make her slump that way?

"OK, Mr. Johnson," she said, still looking down at the notes she had made. "You'll be contacting a Dr. Steven Goldstein at UCLA Medical Center in Los Angeles," she continued. "I wrote down some reference numbers that might come in handy." She handed him the sheets of paper. The faint sound of a back door shutting could be heard as she finished. "Our office is about to close, so if you have any questions, feel free to call in the morning. We'll be open at eight."

"Yes ma'am," he said, as he made his way out the door.

It'll take at least two weeks of good hard work just to begin to catch up. And that's if he can stop by at least twice a week…He's been a good neighbor, but this just may be asking too much…I don't know how I can repay him. Money's not enough for the time I'm taking him away from his farm.

His thoughts were interrupted by the thunderous sound of a commercial jet leaving the airport. The pain pills he had taken before landing started to take effect. A steady flow of vehicles of different sizes, colors and shapes jockeyed for position as they repeatedly looped the loading zone. The one vehicle of importance, the airport shuttle, swung in for him and his luggage. In a matter of minutes, they were out of the airport and on their way.

Not willing to stray from his scheduled route, the driver stopped a couple of blocks from Robert's hotel. As if to compensate for not bringing him closer, he jumped out and quickly helped him with his luggage.

Once unloaded, he noticed three derelicts a block ahead, two propped up against the wall of an old storefront, the other, the farthest away, asleep on a broken down cardboard box.

In the back of his mind, second thoughts arose about letting Dr. Hendrickson's secretary make hotel reservations.

As he approached the three men, a strong smell of beer, body odor and urine hit him all at once. He thought he heard one of the men mumble something.

To Robert, a lean, rugged mid-western farmer, these men posed no physical threat but something inside made him feel sorry for the waste of life. What makes these men so different from me?

As he started to step over the third and final man, his foot was met by a distinct buzzing sound. Fear quickly overtook him. Looking around nervously, he knew there was no place to hide, no escape from the seizures that always followed the sound.

His entire world narrowed to his immediate surroundings. Just him and the three transients…

Suddenly the fear was compounded by a new fear. The inevitability of the event was solidified with the loss of control of his body.

As droplets of water hitting a windowpane converge, so was the transition of the present into the world of memories:

The early sixties. Two boys growing up in a trailer park in Northern California. A single mother struggling to feed her sons.

Next, the thought of childhood friends flow by.

Significant events force their way to the surface. There is the image of a mother. My mother, standing in the door of our trailer, crying. Two men in military uniform wait to take me away. My teenage brother is at my mother's side. My mother, a forlorn expression, waves to me. It hurts. It really hurts.

A wave of new images arrived, displacing the hurt with fear.

My men and I are pinned down behind enemy lines. We're outnumbered. The screams of two of our own, captured the night before can be heard through the thick of the Vietnamese jungle. A decision is made. I make it. Fight our way out no matter what the cost. Most of my men are lost. A handful of us escape - but with just our lives.

Years of trying to cope pass. My brother's suicide is the final breaking point. Drugs, alcoholism, and finally homelessness are all that remain.

The looming despair was dissolved by a voice. "Mr. Johnson, can you hear me?" A female E.M.T. unlocked a stretcher from the inside of an ambulance. "Come on, you guys, give me some help." She waited for her two male cohorts to assist in unloading the patient. "That's two seizures this week." They lowered the stretcher onto its locking retractable legs. "I believe I've won the pool once again."

"Yeah," replied one of the others. "That will give you just enough money to pay me back from two weeks ago."

"I forgot about that," she said. "Damn drunk driver. If only these people knew we had money riding on them."

The conversation stopped when a female nurse appeared at the E.R. doors.

"You can put him in trauma room six," the nurse said. She pointed toward the main E.R. area. "Where are all his belongings?" she asked, as the crew started toward the door with the patient. While two of them maneuvered the stretcher past her into the E.R, one of the male attendants handed her a plastic bag that contained a wallet. "This is all he had with him," he said, as he trailed his two colleagues inside.

Regaining his bearings Robert, quickly realized where he was. Raised padded side rails restricted his side-to-side vision but allowed him to see toward his feet. A large sliding glass door muffled the sounds of daily hospital activities.

As he tried to pull himself together mentally, his visual attention was soon snared by the sight of a man, maybe in his late forties, sitting in a wheel chair outside his room. All of the activity going on around had no effect on him. He sat there, motionless, head shaven, tilted forward and slightly to the right. He wore a hospital gown. Resting between his legs was a straight white cane rounded off at the end with a black strap at the top. Two more people passed and still he didn't move.

What in the past would have been just a curiosity for Robert now became a need; a need to know and understand. He knew something about him had changed. He noticed it after the first couple of seizures. After each experience, he felt a growing desire to interact with the people whose life's memories seemed to coexist with his own; to share something with them. Something he could feel but something that was impossible to articulate.

Another difference he noticed. If from the trauma or some side effect of the medication he was taking, he now thought more in-depth about what would normally be everyday events.

A young slim nurse, slowly sliding the door to his room open, instantly eclipsed the image of the wheel-chaired man. Dark black hair disappeared into a ponytail behind her back. The clean dark blue scrubs she wore where pressed perfectly.

"Hello, Mr. Johnson," she said, closing the door behind her as she entered the room. "My name is Sharon." She moved to the right of the gurney, establishing once more his view of the man outside. "They said the line they started in the field was no good, so I need to start another one. I'll be right back. It'll just take a minute. Your wallet is in that bag on the shelf above your head."

Robert looked up at the shelf, then back at the nurse. "Where's my luggage?"

"What luggage?" she asked.

"I just flew in from Kansas. I had luggage."

"I'm sorry, Mr. Johnson, but this is all they said you had with you."

"Did you ask the three bums?" he inquired, at a loss for a better way to describe them.

"I can ask again, but I'm pretty sure they said there were no bystanders." She leaned forward, resting both of her hands on the bed railing. If you think that something of yours has been stolen, we can call the police now or you can wait until you're discharged to fill out a report. Since you're a visitor I'll give you directions to the nearest police department." She straightened back up. "That's if you'd like to wait."

"It's OK," he said, still looking at her.

"It's OK?" she asked, seeking clarification.

"I'll wait," he replied. He turned his attention away from her and back to his view outside. "They just don't realize how it affects others to take things that aren't theirs."

"I know what you mean," she said, not knowing whether he was talking to himself or to her. "It says in the bible, 'Thou shall not steal.'"

Still staring outside, he responded softly, "Everyday life tells you the same thing. You just have to be willing to listen and learn."

Before she had time to reply, he asked, "What is that man outside here for?"

"Oh, Fred," she said, taking a quick look. "He works here. I mean, normally he works here. He had a problem on the job so he had to be seen. I'm not sure what for, not that I could tell you anyway. I know once he ran into someone and fell. Of course, he didn't see the person coming. I guess that cane can't detect moving objects.

"He's blind?" Robert asked, looking back at her.

"Yeah, they're pretty good about hiring the handicapped here."

"What does he do?" he asked.

"You mean, where does he work?"

"Yes."

"Radiology."

"He takes x-rays?"

"No, no. He has something to do with film developing." Realizing that her answer might only spark more questions that she didn't have time to answer, the nurse decided to cut the conversation short. "Let me run out and grab an IV tray and I'll be right back." Shortly, she was outside, sliding the door closed behind her.

Robert tried to relax his mind. He slowed his breathing. As he lay there looking up at the ceiling, the pain in his leg made him take into account that, with the loss of his luggage, he also lost his medication. He would remember to mention that to the nurse when she returned.

As the sands of the desert accept the harsh rays of the sun, so too had Robert learned to accept this condition. To accept the helplessness that went with it. To accept the loss of control. To accept the buzzing sound that was now rushing up around him, resonating off the walls of his room. He accepted and let go…

His sense of smell, touch, taste and hearing were instantly heightened. What would have been affirmed by visional memories was now replaced by magnified versions of his remaining senses.

The sounds of a younger sister playing in the sand in front of our beachfront home in Santa Barbara. Her giggling voice calling my name. She's seven. I'm nine. I'm sitting on my favorite rock, facing the ocean. I can hear the crisp sound of waves pulsing forward, probably ten to fifteen feet in front of me, then sliding back into that vast body of water that I've been told extends for miles. A dry warm breeze touches the right side of my body and in a constant flow moves over me, swirling away, off to my left. The voice of our mother calling us for dinner grounds my thoughts. I waited for my sister to lead me inside.

The memories moved on.

Now, I'm twenty and a part of me has been lost. Something dear. She's gone away to college and left me here, alone. She calls to check on me but it's not the same.

My parents soon help me find a job at a local hospital, developing film in the dark room of their radiological department. It's automated. It's easy work. It helps.

Years later I meet someone who fills that void created by loneliness. Her physical shortcomings don't matter. What matters is that she cares for me and I care for…

"It looks like he's starting to come out of it. Sharon, did you get a history or list of medications he's on before he went under?"

"I haven't had time," she replied, looking back at a tall silver-haired doctor standing at the door. "But I think my LVN took some orders from Dr. Kasselman before he went to lunch." Still talking, she sat a tray on the patient's bedside table and walked toward the door. "I left for just a minute to grab an IV tray and I get back and he's seizing." She started to move past the doctor and out the door. "Let me grab his chart," she said, "and I'll be right back, Dr. Jacobs." Talking aloud to herself, her voice tapered off. "I've got too many patients." At once, she was gone from view.

Moments later she returned with the patient's chart to find the doctor had moved on to a more critical case. She laid the chart down on a counter against the wall. To her relief, the patient seemed to be better. "So how are you doing?" she asked, straightening his sheets. "You had a little episode while I was gone. Raising her voice slightly, she asked again. "Mr. Johnson, are you alright?"

As if talking to no one, not even himself, he spoke. "I think…" he hesitated. "I think I understand."

"You understand what?" She stopped what she was doing to listen.

Looking out at the area that was once occupied by the wheel-chaired man he answered. "I think I understand what's happening to me."

"You're having seizures," the nurse said, pulling a stool up to his bedside. "So what I need to do is get a line going on you so we can push some meds."

Robert, still staring outside, spoke with a misty detachment. "At first, I thought there was some mental connection between me and whoever was around when I would seize. But now I know that's wrong. So wrong. There's no mental connection. No ESP. What's happening to me is what happens to everyone who goes to sleep at night. I'm just dreaming about the last thing I see before I seize. Somehow, my condition is creating some sort of intense elaborate dreams. They just seem like memories." He said something to himself that the nurse was unable to discern. "But feel like…memories."

Not knowing how to respond, the nurse sat there for a few moments. Something about what he was saying made sense. It seemed almost right. But reality, her immediate reality, rejected the idea. Her mind categorized and labeled the knowledge, then pushed it away. "That's very philosophical," she said. "I had to take some philosophy in college. Too bad I've forgotten most of it or we could talk." Movement outside the room drew her attention.

Dr. Jacob walked up to the door and slid it open. He stuck his head in. "Sharon, when you get that line going, hang a bag of normal saline at about two hundred cc's an hour. Get him on some high flow O2 by mask. Also, try to get a better history on him. If he's taking Dilantin, give him about a gram. Go ahead and get a Dilantin level and some lytes on him also." He started to close the door then stuck his head back in. "Since we don't have a good history, throw a urine tox screen in there also. Thanks, Sharon. I'll write the orders." He moved away, leaving the door open.

"You heard him," the nurse said, turning back to Robert. "Lets get started."

When she attempted to position his right arm, he gently pulled it back, reached up and placed his hand on her shoulder. "I would like to leave now," he said, still touching her.

"Are you sure?" she asked. "We've just started to treat you."

"I'm sure."

"You'll have to sign yourself out AMA"

"What's AMA?"

"Against medical advice."

"If that's what I need to do." His hand slowly slid off her shoulder and fell back to his side. "Sharon," he said, "the reason I came out here is to be seen by a specialist at UCLA. I should be able hold to out until then."

"Would you like us to contact that physician?" she asked, trying to help.

"It won't be necessary," he replied.

"We could arrange for a transfer."

"That won't be necessary."

"We could confirm your appointment."

"Sharon," said Robert, attempting to put an end to her efforts. "You've been very helpful but all of the arrangements have been made. I need those directions to the nearest police station."

"Well, she said, "let me run out and get the forms you need to sign. When I get back, I'll give you directions." She started to leave.

"Sharon," said Robert, stopping her at the door.

"Yes?"

"Thank you."

* * * * * * I V * * * * * *

"Jessica, don't push me!" Lieutenant Rawlings said, defiantly glaring back at his estranged wife seated across from him. Like a silent mediator, a large metal desk, disheveled with paper work was all that separated the two.

Jessica began to speak but held back as a young sergeant walked in and placed something on Lieutenant Rawling's desk. She sat motionless, her dark brown dress flowing over her arms, chest and legs, almost touching the floor. Because of her lack of movement, her soft black, shoulder length hair had a stiff appearance. Her sharp angular features, soothed by olive colored skin remained expressionless. Dark green eyes glared back at the man she once loved; ten years her senior, evenly graying hair and slightly overweight body. A light blue short-sleeved shirt, top button undone and a partially loosened black and white old-fashioned tie completed the picture.

How could I have fallen in love with a man like this?

They waited for the sergeant to leave.

Grabbing the moment to respond, Jessica spoke. "Don't push you or what? You'll hit me again?"

"Damn it woman," the Lieutenant shot back, visibly holding back anger, "I said I was sorry." He quickly looked around for eavesdroppers, then continued, "Don't embarrass me in front of my men. We'll talk about this some other time."

"David, you've drawn this out too long as it is. Are you going to sign the papers or not?"

Holding down his voice he responded, "My lawyer says…"

"Your lawyer!" Jessica forcefully interrupted. "My lawyer said not to give you a chance to breathe. But because of what little feelings I have left for you, I'm giving you fair warning." As if lecturing to a child, she slowed her speech. "Get your act together or I'm going to take you for everything you've got!"

"You're entitled to half," he replied, "and that's all you're getting."

"That's just like you, David. Always overlooking the important things. Have you've forgotten visitation rights? Have you forgotten custody? Have you forgotten that you have a son?"

Pent up anger forced the Lieutenant to his feet. "You fucking bitch! You wouldn't dare!"

"Try me."

Calming himself the Lieutenant settled back into his chair. "Give me a week and I promise…"

Jessica cut him off again. "Two days."

"What?"

"You've got two days."

When she stood to leave, he followed. "Honey, wait," he said, extending his hand, as if to summon her back. "Jessica." He stopped and tried one last verbal attempt. "Honey, please."

As she vanished out the front door of the department, the lieutenant's anger resurfaced in the form of a clinched fist pounding a nearby desk. "Fucking bitch!"

He stared in her direction for a minute.

"Lieutenant?" The same young sergeant approached him.

"What?"

"We've got a medical emergency developing outside."

"What is it?"

"Some guy's going into convulsions or something at the front steps."

"Did you call an ambulance?"

"Yes sir. They should be here any minute."

"Good Sergeant. You handle it but keep me posted. I've got some phone calls to make."

"No problem, Lieutenant," replied the sergeant sharply as he walked toward the door.

Sirens could be heard in the distance as the Lieutenant made his way back to his desk, sat down and started flipping through his Rolodex.

What Robert believed to be anomalous thoughts likened to the fancies of the mind while sleeping, became more and more akin to memories--of his own.

I'm so alone. If only I could find someone to be there for me; some-one to hold my hand when I need support. Will I ever find a man that will give me the understanding and respect I deserve as a woman--as a human being? I don't want to grow old alone. But if I have to, I will. All the signs were there. Why did I refuse to see them? The episodes of senseless uncon-trollable anger building month after month, until the true David escaped. The man I really married. The wrong man for me.

Robert's mind was engulfed by the hurt and pain of thoughts so simi-lar to his own, but at the same time completely different.

He could feel the desire to return to his youth as a young girl with dreams of a future with the perfect man. He remembered a mother who had made her marriage work, no matter what the cost.

With the memory of becoming a woman also came the necessity to sacrifice and to settle. To give up something that all women hold dearly…their dreams.

The intensity and longevity of this episode was greater than Robert had experienced in the past…so much so, that not only was he remembering events up until the trigger point, but beyond.

He could remember a long drawn out custody battle with an abusive ex-husband, and the confused innocent questions of a five-year-old little boy.

Just as Robert started to adjust to the extended memories, the inexpli-cable happened. It all stopped.

Locked in this world of remembrance he could see himself as a thirty-year-old woman named Jessica Rawling, standing outside her Simi Valley home. Awakened by a phone call just minutes earlier, she found herself ner-vously fumbling through her purse for her car keys in the dead of night.

Simi Valley Hospital. I thought it was just a sleep over. How could he have gotten hurt? And damn it, why didn't she call me first?

He could feel the overwhelming sense of responsibility that only a mother could have for her child. All thoughts were focused on getting to her son.

As her hand found that one thing that was holding her back, the car keys, something inconceivable happened…a loud popping followed by her right shoulder jerking forward.

Staggering, her body fell against the car-------Bang! -------Just when she realized she had lost the use of her right arm, she felt something penetrate through the middle of her back, breaking the window in front of her. With each breath she could feel air sucking through her chest. Everything seemed to go quiet, except the sound of an automobile idling behind her.

With only strength enough to lift her head, she looked out into the darkness, her last view of life. My son…alone…who is doing this to me…could it be…David…no…why? Her final thoughts come to pass…her swan song.

Pain and the realization of what was happening welcomed that final bullet-------Bang!-------The force slammed her head back against the car. The dark of night and the darkness of death became one and the same.

Drained by what he had just experienced, Robert found himself lying on his back, cold cement stairs running perpendicular to his body. Silhouetted by the midday sun, two paramedics in blue uniforms stood over him. One, tall lanky and well groomed, was carrying a short wooden board. The other, of average height with a military style haircut, held a bright orange plastic box.

The one with the box leaned partially over, allowing the rays of the sun to strike Robert's face. "Sir, my partner and I are here to help you, if you could just hold still for a minute."

"I'm OK." Robert said, propping himself up on an elbow while shielding his eyes with one of his hands. "I have a seizure disorder. I'll be OK."

"Sir, we're just here to help you," the one with the box said as he crouched next to Robert. "If you think you're fine, then you're welcome to go. But we need to ask you some questions and have you sign a quick form before you do."

"A.M.A.," Robert said, to reassure the two that he wasn't new to the procedure.

"That's correct, sir. Now if you could tell us your name and how you got here."

"My name is Robert Lewis Johnson, and I'm here to fill out some type of police report for my luggage that was stolen."

"That's good, Mr. Johnson. Now can you tell me what time it is?"

As the paramedic carrying the short board moved away the additional sunlight gave Robert an answer. "I don't know, about noon?"

"Uhmm, damn close," said the paramedic. "My buddy's getting that form for you to sign, then we're going to get you inside."

Visibly short of breath, Robert struggled to his feet. "Is there an officer Rawlings working today?" His voice was burdened with the multitude of problems facing him.

"Hang on," replied the paramedic. "Hey!" he shouted to his partner, who was on his way back. "Is that guy Rawling working today?"

"How the hell would I know. What do I look like, his bed buddy?" He handed his partner the clipboard and walked away.

Robert scanned and signed the form.

The Paramedic directed him by placing a hand on his back. "What you can do is ask inside" he said. He stopped at the door allowing Robert to go in. "I'm sure one of the officers will be able to answer any questions you may have." Still talking, the paramedic started to walk away. "Take it easy, Mr. Johnson."

"Thanks for your help," answered Robert in a low voice as he limped into the station.

Inside, a long open space with russet marble tiles extending sixteen to twenty feet from the door buffered the incoming traffic. The interior design was that of an oversized hallway with no windows, but sufficiently lighted. He slowly made his way toward a long counter with bulletproof glass rising from its center.

Everything around him seemed vaguely familiar, like a distant memory. He peered past the glass and saw two rows of desks that he knew would be there. He caught a glimpse of a gray-haired officer in a light blue shirt speaking on the telephone, just as he felt someone place a hand on his shoulder.

"Good afternoon, Sir," said a fair-skinned uniformed officer with short ash blonde hair. "You must be the guy who was having trouble outside a minute ago."

"That's me," Robert replied, noticing what he thought were sergeant stripes on his short-sleeved shirt.

"Good," said the officer. "I mean, too bad that you had the problem, but, good that you seem fine now."

As the officer spoke, Robert's attention slowly migrated back to the gray haired man at the desk.

"One of the paramedics told me you where here to fill out a report," the officer said. He glanced over to see what had his interest. "Is that correct?"

As if caught daydreaming, Robert turned back to the officer and answered, "Yes, yes. That's correct."

"Are you sure you're OK, Sir?"

Robert pulled his thoughts back to the officer. "I'm fine. Just tell me what I need to do."

"Well first," said the officer, "you need to have a seat over there at that desk. Then wait until I dig up our receptionist. She can bring you the forms that you need to fill out." The officer took a few steps away, stopped, turned, and took a half step back toward Robert. "Oh, yeah, if you start having any more medical problems just let us know, before it gets too bad."

He knew his condition was uncontrollable but acknowledged the officer anyway. "Yes, I'll do that."

Robert sat down just long enough for the officer to leave. Within minutes he was outside waving down the first taxi he could see.

* * * * * * V * * * * * *

The night was still and quiet with a starlit cloudless sky. Robert knew that this was the time and place he had envisioned, the night that the young woman whose life he had seen so vividly during his last seizure, would come to an end.

But the fact that he was there, an interloper in the scheme of events, meant something. At the very least, it meant a more intimate understanding of what he was seeing…and experiencing. At most, he could only pray that his mere presence would break the chain of scenarios that would lead to this Jessica's death.

Robert stood in the street, looking over the house. It was exactly how he knew it would be, a two-story brick structure built in the early eighties.

Any minute she would emerge and walk to her car. Robert's heart began to beat faster in anticipation. In the distance, the faint sound of a slow moving vehicle could be heard getting closer. Robert stepped behind a mini van that was parked nearby. The approaching vehicle moved into view and stopped with its driver's side facing Jessica's house and its engine still running. The late model Chrysler sedan had windows tinted so darkly that Robert couldn't see inside, though he squinted and strained to look through the ominously shaded glass. That is not David's car. He thought to himself. Who could be driving…?

Suddenly the door of Jessica's house flung open and she emerged. She slowed long enough to shut the door behind her, then walked to her car. Robert glanced over at the black Chrysler just in time to see the driver's side window lower. He started running toward Jessica, who was now at her car's door fumbling through her purse for her keys. When he reached her, she was so startled by his sudden appearance she dropped her purse and screamed.

"No, wait!" said Robert, holding up both hands "I'm here to…

Bang!

Robert felt a sharp thud against his left shoulder, forcing him forward against Jessica. He grabbed her clothing with his right hand dragging her to the ground and dropping to his knees.

"Oh my god!" said Jessica. "Who are you?"

Robert, still on his knees and trying to catch his breath, reached up and touched his hand to his left shoulder, then looked at it. It was covered in blood. "My name is Robert," he said in a low labored voice. His body swayed back and forth. "I was walking by and saw a man with a gun."

Bang!

Jessica's driver side window shattered sending pieces of glass raining down on them. "Your phone," said Robert. "Call 911, and stay down… No…No…Not now!"

His words were met by something he had become all too familiar with. No matter how hard he tried, the sound of buzzing overtook any will power he had. As his mind slipped away, he could hear the faint sound of a gun firing in the distance.

Before he knew it, the landscape of events had completely changed.

So much sadness.

So much sadness enveloped him that he welcomed the jealousy and anger that followed.

He was a young boy in Whittier, California. He was alone…again…at home. His mother was gone. Out late, drinking, somewhere.

The memories jumped.

He's in high school now. He's not an athlete, but he tries. The girl he offers his feelings to gives hers to another. With these memories, Robert could feel the jealousy and anger intensify.

Though the thoughts he was experiencing leaped forward, the feelings lingered.

Now he was a member of a local police department and the feelings of his past had found a new focus. Like tentacles, they attached themselves to the ex-wife of one of his superiors.

Time flickered on.

The sadness reappeared in its full glory as the jealousy and anger were forced aside. A mysterious man and a botched murder attempt replayed in his mind. Freedom lost…

Prison bars separate him from the outside world.

Like a powerful gust of wind, a burst of light instantly blew away the negative emotions that had been bombarding Robert's awareness. A new scene far removed from the person's life he was just living, immediately replaced the void.

Now he was himself, Bob Johnson, standing in the middle of a wide-open field. All around him were carousels, merry-go-rounds with wooden horses spinning in circles round and round. One of them was brighter then all the others and had a giant red bow tied to its top like a present or…gift. Robert walked over to it and stepped onto its rotating platform. He became dizzy. "This is my life," he spoke under his breath. "It can't be…It can't be. Our bodies are the wooden horses, repeating themselves…the same scenarios over and over. Our souls jump from merry-go-round to merry-go round. The lightening knocked me off…the seizures caused me to remember. I've lived their lives. Her future was my past. Oh my god!"

"Jessica!" Fighting his way back into the present, Robert struggled to regain control of his mind and body. "Run!"

"Mr. Johnson. You're allright. You're at Simi Valley Hospital."

A female voice pierced the fog that had clouded his awareness.

"Where's Jessica?"

"Your girlfriend? She's right outside talking to the police."

"The police?"

"Yeah they caught the guy that shot you. You're lucky the bullet only grazed your shoulder."

Robert heard what she said but didn't feel a need to respond. Instead, he mumbled something that the nurse tried but could not comprehend. "Her future was my past. I was her before she was her. The memories…all of them…are mine."

"Well," said the nurse. "Make yourself comfortable. I'm Cindy. I'll be your nurse and I'll be back in a little bit." She handed him a cord with a red button at its end. "Just push this call button if you need anything." She walked over to a large sliding glass door. Before leaving she turned to Robert and said, "You didn't want to be out tonight anyway. It looks like it's going to rain."

Robert turned his head just enough to see through a nearby window.

Outside…

in the distance…

gaseous water molecules ascended toward the heavens…

TERRA

A large black crow balanced on a tree branch high above some thick swamplands somewhere in North America. It watched as two men in black trousers and white, short-sleeved button down shirts entered a clearing. The older of the two carried a large bag with the ends of an ax and shovel hanging out of it.

Minutes passed.

The young agent stopped and kicked a clump of soft wood-like material with black hair and thin fibers dangling from it. He looked up at his senior officer. "What the fuck is this?"

"Just keep diggin'," the older man said. "You'll learn soon enough. I'll tell you what," he said with a grin. "You keep diggin' and I'll fill you in as we go."

The rookie agent scowled, then split the air with the hard overhead swing of a pick ax.

The veteran agent looked around for eavesdroppers, crossed his arms and spoke while staring at the shallow hole the rookie had created.

"Ya know boy…" He stopped, coughed up something in his throat then spit into the hole, "You should consider yourself lucky."

The rookie glanced up at him, then continued digging.

"Damn lucky. Most people go through their entire lives not knowing the truth." The older man unfolded his arms, scratched his crotch then folded them again. "Hell! Most people wouldn't know the truth if it hit 'em right in the face!" He started to unzip his pants. "Boy, turn around for a minute."

The rookie straightened up with a questioning look on his face. "What?"

"I gotta take a damn leak; now turn around."

He turned resting his hands on the long handle of the pick ax. Behind him he could hear the sound of his superior relieving himself on the ground.

"Don't worry boy. I'm not gonna hit ya. Years of practice."

"You done yet?"

"Yeah, I'm done."

He turned and saw a crisscross pattern of pee in the hole he was digging. "You're an artist," he said, stopping to admire his partner's work.

"A god damn Picasso," answered the older man, readjusting his belt. "Now keep digging. I wanna get the hell outta here some time today."

He continued with a few more swings of the ax before laying it down and walking over to where a shovel and a container of water were sitting. Three big swallows went down before he stopped to offer the other man what was left.

"Want the rest?" He held the water out toward him.

"What the hell," the older man answered, gesturing for him to toss over the bottle."

The rookie threw it to him and watched as he rapidly finished off what was left, then flung the empty plastic as hard as he could into the distance.

"Hot, ain't it?" the older man said, wiping moisture from his mouth.

"Too hot," the rookie replied, as he picked up the shovel and made his way back to the hole. He stopped beside his work to take a breather.

The older man pointed toward the hole. "Dig!" The force of his voice stressed his seriousness. The young agent immediately started removing the dirt that was loosened with the pick ax. A minute or two passed when the older man abruptly blurted out something for no apparent reason. "Screw 'em."

Still digging, the young agent looked up with sweat covering his face. "What?"

"Screw the bastards. If people were so interested in the truth they'd be actively looking for it. It's not like what we're doing is hiding anything from them. The truth is all around us, plain and simple. If they're not drawn to it, then they're not meant to have it. Stupid sons of bitches."

The younger man stopped to listen but was verbally pushed on by the other.

"Dig! Did I say stop digging, god damn it?"

The shovel sliced through another layer of loose dirt.

The older man continued talking as the younger one toiled at the job at hand.

"If you handed civilians the truth, they wouldn't know what to do with it anyway. It'd be wasted. Kinda like giving someone who's never had money sudden wealth. It's not a gift to be given but something that has to be earned. Tempered by experience. You wouldn't give a bum off the street a million bucks would you?"

Obviously not expecting a response he answered his own question. "Of course not. So screw 'em! Screw 'em all!"

The young agent's body seemed to be moving mechanically. He was visibly tired. With each scoop of the shovel he appeared to become more withdrawn from his surroundings and increasingly connected to what he was doing.

Digging…

The older man was saying something but most of it the rookie didn't hear.

He thrust the shovel again into the dirt. This time it didn't penetrate as deeply. Not because the lower ground was any harder, but because his body was becoming weaker. He looked up at the other agent and knew he had no other choice but to continue.

Sweat filtered through the chest, back and pits of his shirt. His hands began to tremble. He took a deep breath and focused hard on the ground in front of him. The shaking stopped for a moment then started again. He looked up at his fellow agent, the man who had brought him there.

"I'm tired. How much deeper?"

"I don't give a fuck what you are! Keep digging!"

He lifted the shovel to continue but stumbled to one side.

"I'm about to throw up. I have to sit down for a minute."

"You stop now," the other man said angrily, "and I'll have to take over. And if I have to take over, then I'm the only one leaving this swamp alive."

A startled look came over the younger man's face. He didn't know what to say.

"Dig!"

The young agent reared back and plunged the shovel into the ground with a fearful enthusiasm. The nausea increased. Every time he pulled more dirt from the hole it seemed to get worse. It was as if something he was doing was making him physically ill.

"Feels good doesn't it?" the older man said with a wicked gleam in his eyes.

If the younger agent wasn't questioning his own mental faculties, he could swear that something was affecting his fellow agent.

The older man spoke loudly, as if he knew what the younger man was experiencing; and, in order to be heard, it was necessary to raise his voice.

"From this point on boy, you must wipe away all of the things you've been taught to believe in. You must think entirely for yourself, to question everything and everyone. What you're gonna learn here today is only the tip of the iceberg."

The young agent stopped to catch his breath again. "Why are you doing this to me? Why are we here?"

"We are here, young lad, because the sheep are out of control. This planet was only meant to accommodate a fraction of what the population has become. Resources are being depleted, usable land more and more scarce. Wars help, but if it's not a clean victory, even they can be wasteful and worse, risky to us."

"Us?"

"Think of us as sheepherders. You've heard the stories of a handful of men running the world. Well, some of it's true. But you know what they say about strength in numbers. It's hard to keep so many savages confused and fighting each other."

The younger man looked at his superior with disbelief. "I thought you said that I should question everything and everyone. Why should I believe any of this bullshit you're feeding me?" He spit into the pile of dirt he had created.

"That's why we're here, little man. Someone up top thinks you might be an asset. That could be good or bad. Frankly, I don't give a shit. I'm just here to do my job and go home. So, if you could do us both a god damn favor and continue digging, I'd appreciate it."

The veteran agent pulled his gun from its holster and held it to his side. The rookie responded by lifting another shovelful of dirt from the deepening hole.

"You see boy," said the older man, still speaking loudly," for the past ten years there have been some unusual earth changes that mainstream science hasn't been able to explain. But we have. It's been a gradual buildup of events. Storms, floods, droughts and even earthquakes. All signs. Soon, you'll learn that nature can be not only an obstacle to progress but to our very survival.

Now with each shovel the rookie could feel a dull aching sensation in his right forearm.

"You see boy, there's a field of energy that surrounds the planet. We've been monitoring it for some time. And that's what brings you and me here." He chuckled in a crazed manner.

The pain in the younger man's arm was becoming worse. Yet he knew he had no other choice but to continue.

"I'm no scientist but since I've had to explain it to greenies like you a few times, I've got it down."

The ache in his arm began to splinter and increase.

"About twice a year that energy field intensifies and narrows at different locations around the globe. Unlucky for us, it's usually in some god damn swamp like this or the middle of some fucking rain forest. We've come to the conclusion that as far back as the last twenty years or so most of the large scale disasters represent some sort of communication."

The rookie was too caught up in what was happening to him to hear the other man's last sentence. He stopped digging, not to hear better what was being said, or because of the strange sensations that were now pulsing through his body, nor to regain enough strength to continue digging, he had stopped because the shovel appeared to have met its destination.

Confused and exhausted he dropped to his knees. The strangeness of it all clouded his senses.

"What we have here," said the older man, "is another attempt at communication. A liaison between it and us."

"What in the hell is this?" said the rookie still kneeling next to the hole he had created. He looked down at a piece of soft light brown rubbery material. Mesmerized he slowly reached down and touched what his shovel had unearthed. "Is that flesh?"

"You ain't seen nothin' yet, boy. The first one I cut up left me sick for a week. The longer you wait, the more it's gonna hurt."

The younger man's body began to sway back and forth. He could feel his heart beating faster.

"You see, boy, this is the center of one of those energy disturbances we've been tracking."

The rookie tipped forward trying to get a better look at what was inside the hole. He spoke softly under his breath. "Is that…a…human…body…?" He squinted. "Is it a…man…woman…What the…" Feeling his heart beating faster, he put one hand to his chest.

"What you're feeling, we think, is some type of defense mechanism. It's trying to survive, and that is something we cannot allow. They tell me, if one of these things were to grow, it would look human…female, they think…figures."

The rookie's entire reality had shifted into a fogged stupor. The only thing that seemed to matter was the hole before him. Again, his body swayed forward. Each time, he would catch himself before falling over. "I feel its…pain."

"Kill It!"

The rookie reached down and rubbed his hand over what was in the hole. "When I touch it, it's as if I'm touching a part of myself." As he moved his hand across the material in the hole, he could feel the impression on his own arm.

"Kill it now! That's an order!"

A feeling of impending doom engulfed the rookie's body, not from anything happening around him but on a larger scale. He spoke under his breath. "So much suffering…so much hatred."

"God damn it, boy!" The veteran yelled. "I'm giving you one chance to make it outta this fucking place alive!" Gun in hand, he moved next to the kneeling rookie. He placed the weapons barrel against the rookie's temple. "Start chopping or I'll blow your brains clear across this swamp, you piece of shit!"

"We can't…we can't do this."

The older agent kicked the rookie hard out of his way and picked up the shovel.

"Damn you for making me go through this again!" A look of intense anger twisted his face as he started aggressively disfiguring what the rookie had uncovered. With each blow, his body seemed to shiver and jerk with an almost painful discomfort.

The rookie was now on his side. He had managed to crawl a few feet but was overcome by what his body was experiencing. He spoke loud enough for the veteran agent to hear. "You can feel it, can't you?"

"Shut up!" he said. "I'll deal with you in a minute!" His eyes narrowed as intense bursts of hate flavored each swing making them increasingly vigorous. Little bits of flesh-like material speckled his face and shirt, interposed with drops of green and red.

His final blow was punctuated by the deep groan of the rookie agent who was still lying in a fetal position a few feet away.

The older man stopped, his body slumped over, shovel touching the ground. He had trouble catching his breath. A heavy layer of sweat had enveloped his face and was dripping off his chin and infusing the ground at his feet.

For a minute nothing could be heard but a soft breeze rustling the leaves of trees in the distance, contrasted by the labored breathing of the veteran agent.

"You killed a part of us," groaned the rookie, who was curled up on the ground in pain.

Like smoldering embers dowsed by a flammable liquid, the veteran's eyes turned with more hatred burning in them than before. He stared at the incapacitated rookie and walked toward him, shovel in hand.

"You can't..." The rookie struggled to speak.

The veteran agent stopped next to him.

"You can't stop it."

The veteran gripped the shovel tighter. "It's your turn." He lifted it over his head, arching his back to give the first and most devastating blow maximum force....the blow that split through the blur between life and death, severing that fragile tether that connects this world and the afterlife.

Finished, he tossed the shovel aside and spit on his handy work. "Fool," he said out loud. "Since you love it so much, let it consume you!" He turned and started walking back in the direction they had come. Stopping by a tree, undoing his pants to relieve himself again, he glanced up to see storm clouds gathering overhead. "Damn rain." he said, aloud.

Without warning he heard a loud bang. His body was thrust forward. An extreme pain incased his midsection. He dropped to his knees "Shoot me, you son of a..." He tried to speak but only gurgled blood. He reached for the place on his body where he'd been shot. His fingers slid into a large gaping hole where something had passed completely through him.

Stumbling to his feet, he turned back expecting to see the younger agent still alive, but saw nothing. He fell back to his knees as a damp coldness seem to befriend the horrible pain resonating throughout his body.

Slumped and head lowered, each labored attempt to breath brought him closer to the inevitable. With what little energy he had left, he lifted his head as a flash of light burst from the clouds overhead.

Like a giant rod extending from the heavens a bolt of lightening arched down, skewering his torso. He fell face first into the swamp's soft soil and expelled his final breath.

High on one of the swamp's tree branches, a pitch-black crow rustled its feathers and flew off...toward the horizon.

So This is Love?

Imagine this:

Three beings, spheres of energy. Two large and one small. A mother, father and their offspring. What we would consider a young boy. The parents interact only by mental telepathy.

"You did what?" asked the mother. A strong pulse of thought rushed up to, into, and through the father.

"He left it in the park," he thought back, referring to their child, the smaller sphere, whose thoughts were silent. "There was a storm. We had to leave."

"Without the conceptulous?" Her thought projection wasn't as strong this time but still stern and forceful. "You left a child's toy in the animal park?"

"I'm sorry. I thought he had it with him."

"Did you tell park security that he left the toy there?"

"The Watchers?" Yes, we told them but you know they plan to close that park soon, so they didn't seem to care.

Her following thoughts were smooth and flowed with ease. "Animals shouldn't be treated that way. Even if it is just a park. That toy will only confuse them. And if you confuse enough of them, soon they will all become confused. No one wants to adopt a confused animal. They're hard enough to train as it is."

"The storm's energy," replied the father. "We could feel it getting closer. Its electromagnetic field was making us both uneasy. I'm sorry. If I had known, you know I would never have left without it."

The mother's thoughts were quiet for a moment. Both the father and son waited for her to respond. Finally she did.

"We are all going back to get it."

The father shot back a potent reply. "What?" Even the child's energy began to stir.

"It doesn't belong there, so we are going to bring it back."

"But I told you," said the father, "there was a storm."

"Which is probably over by now," the mother replied. "Let's not entangle our thoughts about this." She sent an impression that drew his attention to their son. "Especially now."

"When?" asked the father, guarding his thoughts.

"Now."

In a flash they were all at the park. Though it didn't affect them, the air was thick and heavy from all the machinery used to maintain it and feed the animals.

The animals. They were everywhere. Some healthy. Most living in filth and barely fed. General control of the wildlife as well as population growth was the duty of park security. One of their jobs was to let it reach a certain point, then cut back on the numbers. But it seemed that, since this park was about to close, they had become lazed in their duties. The animals were breeding too quickly, which also explained why so many of them were dying of starvation.

The mother directed a thought to the father. "Why do you visit this place?" She then encapsulated their son into the thought. "And bring our child?"

"Knowledge," he replied. "Just knowledge."

She blocked all other thoughts about the condition of the place and her mate's reason for bringing their son. "So where is it?" she asked.

"Over there." His mind directed her to the other end of the park. In an instant they moved thousands of kilometers to where they had last seen the toy. The area, devoid of wildlife, was an open desert with rolling dunes all around.

The mother directed a blank thought at the father. Then she questioned the accuracy of the location. "Animals cannot survive here."

He answered while sensing for the toy. "You know that park time is different than our time. Thousands of years have passed since we left." His energy perked up. "I've got it!" This time he directed her attention a distance underground. "The land has changed," he said as he pulled the toy up with the power of his will.

The toy was a weave of a multitude of energy fabrics. Gelatinous in appearance but invisible to the eyes of the park animals. It was perceivable in other, subtle ways.

The mother spun it around then flipped it over. "It's on!" She thought to them angrily. "What were you thinking?"

"It's a child's game," the father answered. "How was I to know it was on?"

The mother focused more closely on the toy. "It's set to krempclut. What game is that?"

Instead of answering, the father directed his thoughts to the son who let out a low embarrassed thought burst explaining the nature of the game.

"Hum," she thought to herself. A conundrum. A game for lower logic, energy.

It emits changing background waves masked with an illusionary cover wave. One has to use just enough energy to formulate lower logic, then try to reason through the cover wave to expose the real nature of the background waves.

She increased the force of her next thought. "Do you know what this does to the minds of the park's wildlife?"

The father and son remained silent.

Suddenly, all three sensed something in the distance emerge from behind one of the dunes. One of the park's animals was walking toward them.

The mother realized too late that the conceptulous was still on. The animal in the distance dropped to its knees. She shut it off.

"Are you ready to leave?" thought the father to the mother.

"Wait," she replied. "We have done much harm to this one."

"It's just an animal," said the father. "We have the toy; now we can leave."

The mother moved toward the animal that was now coiled up on the desert sand. "I will clear its mind; then we may go."

The father answered with silent obedience.

The mother moved directly over the disabled animal for a brief moment then back to the father and son. "We may leave now," she said. And in a flash they were gone.

Jesus Rodriguez pulled the steering wheel of the land rover hard to the right, straightening up the vehicle toward the dune he was crossing. He dropped it into low gear and guided it up the dune's smooth side.

At the top, he stopped to get out and stretch, when something caught his eye in the distance. For an instant, he saw a bright flash shoot lines of intense light into the air. Instead of driving to the location, hesitantly he started walking toward the flash.

It felt like an eternity but something kept pulling him in its direction. His body was tired and dehydrated as he neared the top. Before reaching the crest something inexplicable happened. As if complementing the strange pull that had come over him to reach the anomaly, a feeling of euphoria gripped his whole body. His thoughts began to race and were interwoven with intense emotions that cloaked each and every moment. And in that instant, he knew in his heart that he had found what it means to experience...true love.

His faith and all of the love he had felt in his past resurfaced and was intensified. It was as if whatever was behind that dune was the source of... everything he knew to be love.

He lost control of his will and started running to the top. It was so beautiful. He had to see...and have more.

He breached the summit and stood in amazement at what his eyes beheld.

In the distance, hovering a few meters above the desert sand were three angels of the lord. They were so close he could feel the power and the glory infuse his entire being. It was so overwhelming that Jesus dropped to his knees. His mind had now slipped into a state of confused splendor. In his heart he knew that he was blessed to be there in that place at that moment and to feel what it truly means to be alive. Tears raced down his face.

His head hit the sand.

It seemed like days had passed while Jesus lay there, motionless, when suddenly something brought him to consciousness. He opened his eyes to see one of the lord's angels flying over him. The angel had beautiful wings of silver and wore brilliant white clothing, feet of brass and hands of finest gold. The power of god radiated from its entire body.

Jesus started to pray when...

With a force beyond anything he could have imagined, all that he believed himself to be was purged by the angel. Like a dam being released, the thoughts and feelings that had built up by this experience where washed away leaving behind a clarity of thought that was so...alien...to him that, for a moment, he felt like he was someone or something else. That something caused him to reexamine the profound thoughts he had felt moments earlier.

He now knew there was more that binds living beings together than what one calls "love." More than vague misinterpreted emotions. He knew now that feelings are rags compared to this force of life itself. And that thing that binds him to the beggar, the thief or the scoundrel he has never met, meant more then any false illusion of love for mother, father or mate. He knew now that the connection between him and even the lowest of life was stronger then any feelings one person has for another. Love is a shape shifter. A chameleon. A concoction of ignorance. He knew that what binds living beings together is constant. What binds living beings together does not fluctuate. Does not bend. Does not come. Does not go. But is always. Like deranged soul mates, love and interpretations are married, honeymooning in the abyss of ignorance.

What binds all living things together is based in truth. And truth does not have to be interpreted. Because what is true is eternal. And truth is the progenitor before all that is. Before the interpretation.

Before the word. In the beginning.

There was a flash and the angel was gone. Jesus found himself standing alone where he had collapsed. He shielded his eyes from a bright yellow sun that had moved into his field of vision. He began to regain his own thoughts. They resurfaced and meshed with the vision he had received from the lord. With the clarity he now possessed came a sense of duty. A need to help others. For he knew that that day…in the middle of the desert…that he was chosen…

…by god.

Kupenda

A tall, slender officer in plain clothes entered a medium size living room located on the fifth floor of an apartment high-rise. He was greeted by another male uniformed officer of average height. They stood cautiously away from a door located at the other end of the room.

"It's about time. What took you so long?"

The taller officer pointed a finger at the other man. "Remember your sensitivity training," he replied smiling.

"Oh, I'm sorry," said the uniformed officer sarcastically. "Detective Hendricks, how's ya day been?"

"Don't know yet."

"You don't know?"

"It's cumulative, sergeant. I'll let you know at the end of the day."

"What?"

"To me, each day is an event. So until that event has completed itself, I really can't tell you how I feel about it."

"You are so full of shit."

"You know what they say about one man's shit."

"Speaking of men," said the sergeant, "we're it."

"What do you mean?"

"If you haven't noticed, there are five other officers here and they're all women."

They walked over to a nearby window and looked out. One female officer was talking to a woman in a nightgown. Another stood half shielded by a patrol car; her right hand resting on her side arm. They saw the three remaining officers file into the downstairs entrance of the building where they were positioned.

The sergeant gestured out the window toward the officer talking to the woman in the gown. "Will you check out the rack on that little redhead?"

The detective confirmed his partners' observation. "Uhmm, nice."

They eyed their associate for a few more seconds before turning back to the room.

"So what have we got here, sergeant?"

"A domestic disturbance call. The wife." He tilted his head toward the window. "The woman in the gown says her husband locked himself in the study and refuses to come out."

The detective laughed. "Yeah, and?"

"He threatened her with physical harm if she tried to enter."

"Ok." The detective looked uninterested.

"Most important," continued the sergeant, "the wife says the study is where they keep their gun. A nine-millimeter Beretta."

"Now, that's more like it." He looked over the door of the study. "Any history?"

"No criminal history that we know of, but get this. The guy's some kind of archaeologist or something and, according to the misses, he just got back from three weeks in Africa."

"Just got back?"

"Two days ago. And he's been acting very strange ever since."

The detective glanced around then room looked at the door of the study.

"What d'ya think?" asked the sergeant.

"About what?"

"About gettin' this guy outta there so we can go home."

"Have you asked him to come out?"

Not knowing what to say the sergeant's face went blank and his mouth fell open.

"How about we start there," said the detective, walking over to the door.

The three officers who had filed up the stairs entered with weapons drawn and quickly positioned themselves to the side of the study's door.

The detective gave them a hand signal. "Put those away." He knocked twice then whispered back to the sergeant. "What's this guy's name?"

The sergeant whispered back. "Sturgis."

The detective knocked again. "Mr. Sturgis," he said loudly, "my name is Detective Hendricks. I need you to put away any weapons you have on you and step outside with your hands where we can see them."

"Go away!" a man's voice yelled.

"Mr. Stergis, we want to help you. The only way we can do that is for you to come out unarmed."

"Fuck you!"

The detective glanced at the sergeant. "That's a start." He took a step back and spoke at the door. "We can do this two ways. For all of our sakes, I hope you decide on the easy way. No one wants to see you get hurt."

"You try and break this door down and, I swear, I'll blow my god damn brains out!"

"Easy, Mr. Stergis. Let's slow down a little. Can we talk?"

"About what?"

"You obviously have a lot going on. Believe it or not, we're only here to help. So, if we could just talk for a minute."

"Then talk!"

"Face to face, Mr. Stergis. Face to face."

There was a moment of silence.

"Just you. If anyone else tries to come in, I swear, I'll start shooting."

The detective looked back at the sergeant who was shaking his head, mouthing, "Too unstable."

The detective removed his weapon and handed it to the sergeant. "I'll just be a minute."

"It's your call, you crazy bastard."

He tried the door handle. Locked. He stepped back. "Mr. Stergis, I need you to unlock the door."

Seconds later, the handle jiggled and clicked. The detective tried again. The door opened just enough for him to see a dimly lit room with dark brown carpeted floor. Through the slit he could also recognize bookcases with what looked like reference materials filling them.

"Mr. Stergis, I'm coming in," said the detective, before opening the door wider.

Inside was a room that was unquestionably geared toward one thing: Knowledge. Books were stacked on books. He took a couple of steps inside and let the door close behind him. A voice to his left caught his attention.

"Have a seat, officer."

With no choice but to comply he sat down in a wooden chair that faced a man sitting in front of a window. The man was silhouetted by sunlight that slipped through the thin fabric of white curtains pulled shut behind him. The man seemed more relaxed then the detective expected. In build and height, he was average. Nothing appeared unusual about him, except that he was sitting in a chair with a gun in his lap, across from a police negotiator.

The man's body was completely still as he spoke to the detective. "Officer, we've never met but there's one thing I can say about you…"

"What is that, Mr. Stergis?"

"You've gotta have balls to walk into a room were there's a crazy man with a gun."

The detective tried to choose his words wisely. "Are you crazy, Mr. Stergis?"

"You tell me."

"We all have our problems, Mr. Stergis."

"Some, more then others," he replied.

"True." The Detective focused hard on the silhouette across from him. "So how are you, Mr. Stergis?"

"How the hell do you think I am?"

"Fair enough. So why are we here?"

With a kind of intellectual arrogance the man responded. "You're here because I'm here. I'm here because you're here."

The detective smiled. "Is there anything that you want to tell me? Something you want to get off your chest?"

"Are you married, officer?"

The detective shook his head. "No, divorced."

"You're lucky. It won't be as painful for you."

"The divorce was painful."

The man grunted under his breath. "You think?"

"How can I help you?" asked the detective.

"Who'd you come with?"

"I don't understand your question, Mr. Stergis."

"I asked, 'who did you come with?'"

"A couple of other officers."

"I counted seven from the window. Five women and one more of us."

"Mr. Stergis, you've locked yourself in your study with a gun. You've threatened the life of your wife as well as your own. What do you expect?" The detective was trying to speak as calmly as possible. "Mr. Stergis, what do I have to do to get you out of here?"

"Have you ever been to Africa, officer?"

The detective sighed. "I can't say that I have."

"There's so much history there. So much you can learn." The man cleared his throat. "I just got back."

"Your wife told us. You must be very happy to be here."

"I suppose she also told you the type of work I do."

"Yes, she did."

"I've been gone for almost three weeks living in one of the most remote areas of that continent."

"Must have been some vacation."

"Officer, what took me there was a rumor, a well substantiated rumor that a handful of tribesman from a group we thought died out years ago were still alive."

The detective glanced down at his watch.

"Officer, when I'm through you'll wish that my story had lasted a lot longer!"

The detective tensed up. "I'm sorry, Mr. Stergis, I'm listening."

"That's better."

The man sat without speaking. With a gentle reserve in his voice, the detective cautiously acted on the need to break the silence. "Go on, Mr. Stergis."

The man continued his seemingly irrelevant story. "Not only did I find the tribesmen that I was looking for, I lived with them for two of the three weeks of my excursion. And with the help of the two interpreters that accompanied me…"

"Mr. Stergis, you're home now."

Instead of responding the man carried on with his story. "…I quickly gained their trust. Enough so that I was given the opportunity to meet one of their females."

The man took a long deep breath, then continued. "That day three of the tribesman took me to a clearing at the edge of a forest. From that point, I felt something inside myself begin to stir. It was as if a part of me that I never knew existed was being awakened.

"I waited in that field with those men for what seemed like an eternity. I was all but ready to give up. But, just as a soft breeze began to ripen around me, it happened."

By now the detective's eyes had adjusted to the room's lighting. He could make out an average looking man, in his late forties with short, neatly cut hair and a small amount of gray at the temples, dark brown eyes and a tan complexion.

The man swallowed hard then went on. "It was like a morning sun dispersing a hazy sky as she emerged from an opening through the trees. Before I knew it, her full attention was upon me, and, at that moment, I knew that I had met…a woman."

The detective could see a layer of moisture forming on the surface of the man's skin. The man paused for a moment then lowered his head.

"Her mind softly touched my mind. Everything that had happened in my past…all of my plans for the future, were forgotten. All I knew was… where I was. Not at that moment, but where I was in relationship to her. She had become my only sense of measurement.

"I didn't know what else to do so I…I…moved closer." He stopped.

The detective could see tears well up in the man's eyes as he struggled to make eye contact with him.

"Go on," said the detective, trying to sympathize with him.

He did continue. "I never considered myself a spiritual man but the only way I can describe what I felt next was like two souls ice skating on air. It felt so right. So meant to be. I felt my mind being caressed by the… creature's thoughts."

The man took another deep breath. This time he held the air in briefly before releasing it.

"In the way," he said, "that an aroma brings back the memorable taste of something you enjoyed, so does the mere thought of that woman bring back what I experienced that day."

"Why are you telling me this?" the detective asked, keeping his voice as even as possible.

The man leaned back in his chair and chuckled in a deranged manner. "I told you. I met a woman."

"Yes," answered the detective in confused confirmation. "Ok."

"You should be surprised. I'm one of the few men who have."

"Mr. Stergis, if you come with me there are five very attractive young ladies that would love to meet you."

A wrathful expression came over the man's face. He responded angrily. "Officer, would you like to know why you're not leaving here alive?"

In a show of truce the detective raised both hands, palms toward the man. "Now let's just relax for a minute and try and talk this…"

"Shut up!"

The detective fell silent. His focus narrowed to the tightening grip the man had on his weapon.

"Listen to what I have to say and don't speak until I'm finished. Do you understand?"

The detective nodded. He now saw himself as a man temporarily imprisoned in a lunatic's world. What brought this person to this point he could only speculate. Maybe it was something from his childhood, a trauma of some sort, or as he'd seen so many times, the negative effects of freelance pharmaceuticals.

"Detective, I know you think I'm nuts."

"I never said…"

"Sshhh."

Once again, the detective fell silent.

"It doesn't matter. What does matter is while I was there, something was shown to me. Though the members of the tribe I was with were primitive, their ancestors--our ancestors--were advanced. In every way. Three days before my departure, I convinced one of them to take me to a sacred site, a hidden network of caves."

The detective hadn't moved. Everything from the slightest body motion to his breathing, he wanted to keep as neutral as possible, while at the same time watching for any sudden changes in the man's demeanor.

The story proceeded.

"Inside the caverns, I found an unusual form of writing on the walls. It…interacted with one's touch."

The detective shifted in his chair, then was still.

"If I were to describe how the information on those walls was passed on to me as an impression, I may be doing it a disservice. For these were solid impressions. When you hold an object in your hands, you get an impression of how it feels, how it looks, or even how it smells and sounds. These are all impressions on your senses. All I can say is the impressions I felt were more profound. Disturbingly profound."

"Officer, I'll try to make what has already been a long story, brief.

"In our distant past, we were more advanced then we are now. During this period, an outside race of warlike beings stumbled upon our world. A great conflict ensued. In only a six-month period, both sides were devastated. The aliens were almost annihilated. Except for small dispersed groups, humans were nearly thrown back into a stone age. There was wide spread destruction, but we did survive.

"We soon found we had underestimated our enemies' resilience. They introduced something into our water supplies that killed only the females of our species. Once contracted, it rapidly spread from person to person. The delivery was widespread and lethal. Most of our female population was wiped out with a few able to build an immunity to the agent.

"Still outnumbered, the enemy dealt a second and more devastating blow to any chance we may have had of recovering. When I said they were warlike, I meant they saw battle as something to be won no matter what the cost. And most importantly, no matter how long it took.

"A handful of our women the enemy had taken captive during the war were used to introduce hybrid females into the population. The last alien stronghold was overrun, prisoners were freed, including men, women, children, and an unusual amount of baby girls.

The detective's eyes began to wander. What he was hearing blurred in his mind as each sentence from the man sounded like the previous.

"Pay attention detective," said the man sternly.

The detective restored eye contact with him.

The man resumed his story. "By some type of advanced form of genetic manipulation, what they produced were females that, not only looked like and believed that they were normal human beings, but were also capable of reproducing with us, passing the alien DNA to their female offspring. This DNA has a generational trigger. After enough reproductions, it's activated, bridging their genetic memory with their conscious awareness.

"Have you heard of mitochondrial DNA, or mtDNA, officer?"

The detective was shaken out of a stupor. "N…No. I haven't."

"It's passed down by females. I'd suggest you look it up but…" He stopped himself then continued the story.

"Over the expanse of time that followed the pure female population dwindled. The scientists of old became aware that genetic tampering had taken place, but post war conditions left them with little or no resources to research the problem. The subsequent catastrophes that followed left our ancestors with only one choice: To leave what they had experienced to future generations, in the hope that they would gain enough knowledge to act before the alien gene fully manifested itself in what we now call our women."

The detective was mesmerized by what he was hearing. It was some of the best science fiction he had heard in a long time. Before he could think of what to say, the man continued.

"Along with the loss of our true females came the loss of certain attributes that humans once possessed. The two most significant were the ability to sense each other from a great distance and the other, the telepathic connection between men and women. The second ability is something that originated in women.

"Devoid of this deeper bond that should exist between the sexes, nature took it upon itself to take action using the flexibility of the reproductive drive. Like a natural default mechanism, that thing we mistakenly call sexual desire would attach itself to anything to try and get the job done. Ask any heterosexual male who's been incarcerated for a prolonged period of time. Detective, think of a powerful electrical current searching for the shortest route to its destination. Without the proper conductor it becomes nothing more then distorted energy. Like a destructive addiction, or a heightened lust for power or wealth, they are all results of a lack of something that mankind has not had since this small stretch of recorded history. Would you happen to know what that is, officer?"

The detective was silent. He was still trying to digest the man's story. One thing he was certain of was that this man was in need of a type of help that he was not prepared to offer. His main focus was getting out of there as soon as possible. With or without this individual, it didn't matter. He had this gut feeling that his time was up. He knew he needed to answer the man's question.

"No, Mr. Stergis, I don't know what that is."

"Love, officer. In its purest form – in the form of truth. Without that one thing that binds mankind together there can never be true understanding of our fellow human beings. Culture, race and religions are all stumbling blocks. Without our women, we're all doomed."

Silence fell upon the room once more. The detective sat motionless. He waited to see if there was more to the story. This time the man broke the silence.

"Are you ready?"

"Ready?"

"To leave."

"If you're ready, Mr. Stergis." A strange chilling relief came over the detective. He couldn't believe it was almost over.

They both stood. The man handed his weapon over and waited. The detective gestured toward the door. "After you."

The man took a couple of steps then turned to the detective.

"Take note, officer. The reason they let us stay in here so long is because they didn't want to risk injury to their own." He lowered his head. "We've lost so much."

"Are you saying that my fellow officers are some kind of aliens?"

"These beings are waking up to what they really are."

The detective forced a wry smile and again gestured toward the door. "After you."

The man stepped out, holding the door open for the detective to follow. Not until they both reached the center of the room did they notice that all five female officers and the man's wife had crowded into the small area.

The detective glanced around. "Where's the sergeant?"

He had just enough time to look into the other man's eyes when the sound of one of the female officer's weapons discharging forced disbelief into belief. He tried to speak, but realized that most of his lower jaw had been blown away. In an uncontrolled gesture, he dropped to his knees, bowing to the victors of a long war that he never knew was taking place.

Purificateur Des Ames

A star riddled black sky touched waves of sand that moved in one motionless flow dipping beneath hard cement walls, built by man to encage his fellow man. The interior was grey and lifeless. The halls were only dimly lit.

Deep inside, in a small hot room two old wooden chairs sat facing each other. Next to them grey and white robes were tossed in a heap on the floor. A thin faced, muscular caucasian male with short red hair in his late thirties occupied one of the chairs. He was completely nude except for a small white towel draped over his thigh and groin area. His hands were tied behind his back by a thick rope that was attached to the bottom rung of his chair. The man's body was slumped forward and motionless. Sweat made the towel cling to his mid section. Any moisture that wasn't absorbed by the cloth pooled into the seat area or dripped off his nose and chin to form a growing puddle in front of him on the hard floor.

In the other seat was another male, also caucasian, in military fatigues. He sat erect with arms crossed over a black faded T-shirt. His round face was almost hairless, except for thick black eyebrows that almost touched in the middle of his forehead.

A few feet away and to his rear was a third man, a Latino soldier smaller in stature then the other two and also in military fatigues. In his left ear was a listening device with a black wire running from it and down his front, disappearing at his waist. He had short black hair and a face that showed little expression. He stood quietly with his eyes fixed on the naked man.

The seated soldier leaned forward slightly, speaking to the uncovered man across from him. "Ya know it's after midnight and I can pretty much guess you'd like to go home as badly as we wanna hit the bunks. So how about we end all this right now and ya tell us what you were doing in the middle of the desert?" He pointed toward the pile of clothes, "dressed in those rags?"

The man didn't answer.

"You're a tough son-of-a-bitch. I give you that much. But, ya know, you're fightin' a loosin' battle. No one knows you're here and as far as the world is concerned this camp doesn't exist. Which means, it's only a matter of time before you talk." He stood and turned his chair around so that its rear faced the man, then sat down, straddling it, resting his arms on its back. "Sooner or later you're gonna tell us what we want to know. Hell, after we're through, we probably won't be able to shut ya up. So, save us all some time, and tell us who you work for so we can end this."

The man said something, inaudible.

"What was that?" asked the soldier.

"Mistake," said the man under his breath. His body was as far forward as his bound hands would let it go.

"Ya know," replied the soldier, "ya made a mistake and got captured." He clinched a fist, reached out and picked the man's head up by his chin. "Do we need to start another round?"

The man's right eye was swollen shut. His face had numerous cuts and contusions. He answered in a low voice. "I…just…want…home."

The soldier let the man's head drop. "You're strong but not wise."

The standing soldier seemed to respond to something in his earpiece. He cupped his hand over it in order to better listen. "Sir," he said, putting his hand back down.

The seated soldier half turned in his chair. "What, Gonzales?"

"The bag, Sir."

"What did they find?"

"They don't know, Sir. They still can't identify what type of drug it is."

He turned back around. "The pouch you were carrying with the pills. Who were they for?"

"Mine," the man said his voice still low.

"Good, good," replied the soldier. "Now what are they?"

"Food," answered the man.

"Bull shit! What kind of drugs are you on? Or were you there for a pick up and to bring a sample back?"

Again the man didn't answer. His body went limp.

"Talk, damn it!"

Still no answer.

"You tell us what we want to know and I promise to give you one of your pills. If it really is your stuff."

"Sir," said the soldier to the rear.

"What, Gonzales?"

"I think he's passed out."

The seated soldier shook the man's head but got no response. "Damn it!"

He stood and back-stepped away from the chair. "This bastard will talk soon enough. I'll tell you what. Bring this Druggy one of his pills. Then tell one of our female officers to talk to him. Tell her to act concerned. If that doesn't do the trick then it's time for round six." The soldier started to walk out. "This sympathizer better pray to Allah that I don't have to spend another minute of my sleep on him."

The captive bathed in solitude's reprieve in a semi-conscious state. The nourishing darkness lasted for some time, but not long enough to fend off the gluttonous appetite of suffering. Suddenly, the sound of a door opening and the lights being turned on aroused him. He could hear someone approaching but was still too weak to lift his head to see who had entered.

A female's voice touched one of his senses.

"Sir, I'm here to get you out."

He tried to raise his head again but was unable. He could tell from where her voice came that she stopped somewhere between him and the entrance.

"I can tell that you've been through a lot and I can assure you that it's over." The female soldier took a couple of steps closer. "I have the drugs…I mean I have some of the medication you had with you. Maybe if you take this you'll feel better. She walked up close enough for him to see her shoes and pants, black combat boots with camouflage trousers the color of the desert itself. She turned the chair around to its original position and slowly sat down. Leaning forward, she placed a small white paper cup half-filled with water on the floor in front of him, then gently lifted his head and slipped a tiny green pill between his lips. She leaned back down, picked up the water and lifted his head once more to give him a sip. She saw the pill was gone.

"You dropped it," she said, looking down at the floor.

"No," the man said, with noticeably more strength in his voice. "I swallowed it. Thank you."

"Ok," she said slowly. "So these were your drugs."

The man raised his head, then straightened his body in the chair. "The pills are like food," he said, "and they work very fast." He twisted his muscular frame as if coming out of a deep sleep. With his uninjured eye he looked directly at her. She had short, ash blond hair and her jacket matched her pants. He stared but didn't say a word.

As the seconds passed, she became visibly nervous at the eerie silence that overtook the room.

"I am here to help you," she said, calming herself.

"Then please let me go," he answered.

"We're working on that. But you'll have to co-operate with us."

"What do I have to do?" He asked, still looking directly at her.

She smiled thinly. "Just answer a few simple questions and I promise you'll be on your way home."

"I'll try."

The female soldier's nervousness seemed to dissipate as she asked her first question. "So where do you come from?"

"I can't tell you that."

"OK. Then where were you going?"

"Nowhere. I'm here by mistake."

She sighed. "If you don't answer my questions, it'll be harder for me to help you."

"I know. And I'm sorry."

"Let's try again. What is your name?"

"You would best pronounce it 'Derdnik.'"

"What kind of name is that?" she asked.

"I don't understand," he replied.

"What nationality?"

"None."

"We're not getting anywhere. And if we don't get anywhere, then you're not going anywhere. I need you to think hard about your situation."

"I am not from your world."

"Excuse me?"

"I am not from your world."

"Then what world would you happen to be from?"

"I cannot tell you that."

"If you can tell me you're not from this world, then why can't you tell me what world you're from?"

"Because this place is infested."

"I really have no idea what you're talking about and I think I should have cut that pill in half."

"If I reveal too much, even as primitive as they are, your people may find a way to carry that infestation to my land."

"Infestation?" she asked, leaning forward in her chair.

"This place has been compromised for some time."

"I think you've just lost me." She began to stand.

"Leeches," the man said. His good eye narrowed its focus upon her. "I hate leeches."

"Leeches?" she answered questioningly, then sat back down.

"It would be safe for me to speak about your world if that is what you desire."

She slid her chair back a few inches, noting the obvious hard blows he must have taken to his head area. "Try me."

"Most believe this world is beyond help, but I believe that there is always hope. If I didn't, I wouldn't be wasting my time telling you this. I believe your true self can hear me and will benefit from the knowledge that I am about to give you."

"My true self?"

"Your soul or spirit. Your true self and your physical body's unity have been compromised."

"I have a feeling," she said, "that you wouldn't be surprised if I told you that I need more of an explanation."

"Over an expanse of time, this planet has been periodically deluged with disenfranchised spirits. Some exist externally. Others are of the sinister type, for they are parasitic in nature. They wedge themselves between their hosts' true selves and their physical bodies, feeding off the energy that the body produces in everyday life…the negative and the positive."

"At one time, humans on this world had a stronger bond with their true selves than they do now, but a series of global catastrophes disrupted this flow of knowledge and understanding leaving them open for infection. Everything that…"

He stopped as the Latino soldier entered the room. "You finished with him yet?" he asked.

"No," she said. "Just give me a few more minutes."

"Let me know."

She nodded, then turned her attention back to the man. "Make it quick and have a point," she said. "Your time is running out."

He continued. This time there was a note of urgency in his voice. "Everything that your physical body experiences in life is being filtered through these ethereal parasites. Your soul is in one place. Your body is in another. In between are entities that should not be there. Your senses of sight, sound, touch, hearing, taste and many others that you are not aware of are only products of these entities. Your bodies have been almost completely taken over. The carriers have been compromised."

She shook her head in disbelief. "That's a lot for me to digest. I'll try to give it some thought." She sat up in her chair. "So, can you at least tell me who dropped you off in the middle of the desert?"

"I have a ship," he replied.

"And where is this…ship?"

"Where it has always been."

"And that is?"

"Home," he answered.

She sighed.

"We have the technology," he said, "of developing ships capable of creating tangible astral images of themselves and projecting those images with a passenger to remote locations."

"So you're telling me you jumped inside some image of a ship. Rode it here, got out and it - I'm speculating here - disappeared because, of course, it wasn't the real ship, just an image of the ship."

"Yes. My course was laid out but there must have been some type of interference along the way." He looked as if he were reflecting on what happened. "Probably electromagnetic."

"You speak English," she said. "You're wearing Middle Eastern clothing so…" She waited for an answer.

"I speak every language on your planet," he replied. "That and the clothes are a product of the ship. We are familiar with the planets in this region. That information is held in a bank of knowledge that can be drawn upon when visiting any known world. Just before I arrived, my ship tapped that reservoir of information. In a package it familiarized my subconscious with what I needed in order to communicate with the inhabitants here. The clothing is a formless synthetic material that can be manipulated into any type of clothing that I choose." He looked around the room as if someone was speaking to him, then back at her.

"You appear to be in a hurry Mr…what was it…Dirdle?"

"It was Derdnik. When a ship misplaces its pilot it self-corrects and retrieves that pilot from where it left him. It is the pilot's responsibility to be at the pick-up point when the attempt at retrieval is made. The ship will try several times. The first three are in rapid succession. The remaining four are spaced from one month, in your time, to five years." His speech slowed. "I could not survive five years on this planet."

"Let's say I believe you," she said. "What were you intending to do when you got to where you where going?"

"I help others."

"What does that mean, you 'help others'"

"It's my job."

The Latino soldier filled the entrance to the room. "Time's up," he said, looking at them with doubt in his eyes.

The female stood and looked down at the man. "I'm sorry I won't be able to help you but let me make a suggestion." She frowned. "If you still have any of your senses about you, now is the time to start telling the truth." She walked over to the soldier standing at the door. "Hopeless," she said, under her breath. "You must have beat him into insanity."

"We just follow orders," he answered. "Did you get anything out of em?"

"He thinks he's an alien. How much can you get out of someone who thinks he's an alien?"

"We'll find out," he said, then walked back into the room stopping in front of the prisoner, who was now sitting up and alert. "So you think you're from another planet."

There was no answer.

"I suggest that you start talking or beam yourself back up to the mother ship before my superior gets back. If not, you're gonna wish you were on another planet."

The man answered with a clarity that surprised the soldier. "Earth is not the only place where the human form exists."

The soldier bent forward resting his hands on his knees. "If you're from another world, then get yourself out of here."

"It would harm you physically," the man responded.

"Right, right," said the soldier, with sarcasm in his voice. "We've harmed you, so let's see you harm us."

"I believe there is still hope for you."

"I think it's yourself you'd better be worried about."

The conversation was closed by the voice of the other soldier entering the room. "Ah, Mr. Dudley," he said walking up to them, "or whatever she said you call yourself. Looks like we're gonna have to do this the hard way." Without warning he punched the man hard in his midsection. The air rushed from his lungs. His body humped over, then straightened up. "What were you doing in the desert, damn it!"

No answer.

In rapid succession, the soldier started slapping the man back and forth hard across the face. His open hand hit with every other word of his next question. "Who do…you work…for and…what is…your job?"

The last blow sent streams of blood red spit flying from his mouth and splattering across the floor. The man grunted and stared directly into the soldier's eyes.

The soldier angrily grabbed the man by his hair and pulled his head back. "Your job!" he yelled.

A piercing intensity appeared in the man's eyes as he answered, his head still held back by the soldier. "Purificateur Des Ames."

The soldier let go and backed away. "A French agent, huh? Now we're getting somewhere."

"Sir," the Latino soldier spoke from a few feet away. "Would you like for me to see if anyone speaks French?"

"Of course not. This French bastard speaks perfect English…if he is French." He stepped toward him. "What did you say?" asked the soldier, positioning himself for another more powerful blow to the man's stomach.

Just when his fist made contact, something strange occurred. Neither soldier could hear the result of the strike. It was as if the sound in the room had been turned off.

The man humped over, then straightened up, but this time they could see he was mouthing something. Though no sound was being produced, both soldiers knew what he was saying. It was as if a strong impression was filtering into their awareness, forcing a link between the man's mind and theirs.

"My job, you asked," mouthed the man, his body tensing, his eyes staring straight forward, "has a name in your world."

The soldier, who just hit him, took a couple of steps backward. The other soldier was trying to adjust the volume in his earpiece.

"In your world, I would be called…an Exorcist."

The two soldiers, now turned toward each other, tried to talk, but the words found no sound waves to carry them.

"As I strip away the layers of possessions from your spirit, I also take away the senses that connect you to this world."

The lead soldier barked orders at the other soldier but every attempt ended in confusion. He turned back to the captive. Behind him, the other soldier attempted to run, but suddenly collapsed.

"One by one," said the man, still looking straight forward. "I pull away those evil things that have controlled human life on this world for thousands of years."

The soldier that was still standing, lunged at him but his legs gave way in mid-stride. He fell forward, his body hitting the floor hard a few feet from his destination.

"Stripping away the parasites that now control this planet."

Both soldiers felt around aimlessly, dragging themselves across the floor. To them, the room had become completely dark. They found themselves blind and helpless, and somehow at the mercy of a man, naked, bound to a chair.

The man's mind pierced their thoughts one last time. "If you peel away the shell, all that is left is the seed of life. That promise of a new beginning. So, in turn, I discard the negative influences on the marionettes of your physical world."

The two soldiers stopped moving.

"I leave your souls pure. Free from the chains that bound you to this place."

A few minutes later the chair that held the naked man was empty. The bodies of the two soldiers lay sprawled, lifeless, waiting to be discovered.

The Last Hour

G ray, our sensors show you have about sixty minutes worth of air left. Just stay calm while we figure out what to do."

The transmission from earth crackled and hissed but Gray Braxton was still able to understand what was being said. The graceful voice of Julie from mission assurance sounded so reassuring that for a moment he thought she really meant what she was saying. But if they had a plan she wouldn't be wasting his time telling him something he already knew. He tried to slow his breathing and remain as still as he could, using just enough energy to set his personal timer.

Sixty minutes - Set – Notify, every ten.

"Gray." It was Julie again. "You've set your timer for an hour. I suggest that you not do that; it'll only make things worse. You need to stay calm."

A few moments went by with no response. "Gray, can you hear me? Gray?"

A bundle of twisted metal, plastic and wires floated by a few meters in front of him. Sunlight reflected off of the artificial debris as it glided away into deep space. These where among the numerous bits and pieces of what was left of the ship. Five crew-members and tons of modern technology and the only thing that remained was scattered pieces of debris no bigger then a car's door. He had been on an EVA when the meteor hit. No warning. No time to brace for the impact. Not even a moment to think. Somehow the tether was snapped clean without flinging him around which was a miracle. In a split second it was all over. Five lives gone and the sixth hanging onto what little time he had left.

There was a beep…

…a little over fifty minutes.

"Julie," Gray's voice was somber. "I know my time is up."

"Gray…"

He stopped her. "Julie, please." Against his better judgment he took a deep breath. "We all knew this was a possibility. I'm a big boy and if this is how it's got to be, then so be it."

"Gray," said Julie. "I'm sorry."

This time he took a more conservative inhalation. "I just wanna know how you ended up with this duty?"

"I know you have no family and I feel like I'm one of your closest friends."

"Were," he replied.

"What?" she asked.

"You were one of my closest friends."

"Gray, please."

"I'm sorry."

"Don't be."

"You know, Julie…"

"Yes?"

"I always wanted more to be between us."

"I know."

"You knew?"

"Of course."

"Why didn't you tell…?"

This time she cut him off. "Gray, do you know how many people are listening to us right now?"

He answered with a hint of sarcasm. "This is my fantasy, damn it, and I expect you to play along."

"Gray, is there anyone else that you'd like to share this time with?"

"That's just like you, Julie. Personal business stays outside the work arena." He chuckled. "To whoever is listening, you definitely hired the right girl."

"Gray, I'm here to help you."

"It's Ok. I know you are. I mean, what's a guy suppose to talk about in his last few minutes of life?"

Another brief silence.

"You know, Julie, ever since I was a kid I wanted to be an astronaut." He made the next statement with spurious glee. "And look at me now."

There was a frustrated snicker. "All the hours of training, the preparation, the damn simulators have all led me to this. The culmination of my life's dreams.

A low fuzzy male voice could be heard where Julie's had been the only articulation. "He's headed down the wrong path. Julie, bring him back."

"Julie, Julie," Gray responded mockingly. "Are you being coached by psych?"

"Gray, he's only here for advice."

Another piece of the ship's debris floated by. This time he thought he could make out a piece of a crewmate's clothing.

"This can't be happening."

"Gray?"

"I can't be here."

"Gray, please."

"Not me…not me!"

"Gray, tell me what you want me to do and I'll do it!"

"Just leave me alone for a minute or two. That's all I need is just a couple of minutes."

OK Gray, I understand. Remember I'm right here, when you want to talk, I'll be ready."

"I know."

It only seemed like seconds before he heard the next beep. For some reason he thought he had longer. But when there's nothing to compare time to except one's own sense of time, or death, then it all becomes a waste of…time.

He floated there alone…waiting. Just waiting. Trying to rest his thoughts on his breathing proved to be pointless. No matter what he attempted to focus on, or think about, his mind would extrapolate it out until it found its way back to his situation. He thought about how something so abundant on earth could be so indispensable now. It's cheap until you're almost out of it. Then it becomes a priceless yet under-appreciated resource. Rarer then the scarcest mineral. More invaluable then any amount of gold. For this resource…can sustain life.

There was another beep.

My glass is half empty, he thought to himself. Another parcel of wreckage glided about three meters in front of him. This time, intertwined in the twisted remains, he could make out a human arm, torn from its shoulder.

Who was it…one of the four other male crew or was it the one woman among us? His body shivered as a deep sadness came over him. This, he knew would be the time to cry, if there ever was a time to cry. But the sense of futility in his situation prevented the tears that had been amassed by the sorrow, to be released.

His solitude was interrupted by a crackling sound. It was Julie but her voice was hard to make out. He could hear bits and pieces of what she was saying but little else.

"Gray…can't.…solar fla…communicati…"

Then, there was nothing. He listened for a few moments through an even flow of static before he decided to give up. His vision became fixed on a distant star. It's light danced and shimmered through the vast darkness that surrounded him. His mind had become completely mesmerized, until…

He heard another beep.

I just wish, he thought, I had done all the things I wanted to do. Told all of the people the things that I wanted to tell them. He swallowed hard. He took a slow anxious breath. What I've done until now I know will benefit whoever comes after.

He closed his eyes and spoke aloud. "This was not for nothing."

Moisture started to form at the corners of his eyes. He tried to blink it away with no success. If there was gravity, he knew there would have been tears by now. Gray looked for another star to focus on. Something…anything, to take his mind off of the inevitable. He finally settled on one that was similar in brightness to the last.

Gray Braxton gave that star his full attention as he waited for the next beep-the next indication that he was just that much closer to the end of his life. He waited…in silence…in the cold darkness of space…to die.

"We are as you."

"Julie, is that you?"

The quality of the air had changed. He could feel it in his lungs. He halted for a few seconds for a reply but there was none.

"Julie," he asked, "did you say something?"

Still no answer.

Then, again he heard the voice.

"Close your eyes."

It was feminine but not the voice of Julie and definitely not coming from his headset.

"Who's speaking? Identify yourself."

A minute of silence passed before being disrupted by fate's beacon.

Another was a beep.

"Your eyes."

The voice with the same resonance and inflection.

Gray didn't answer, thinking it must be some stray transmission he had picked up. The voice never mentioned him by name and there was no response to his replies.

He quickly concluded that he had been wasting the last few minutes of his life trying to talk to an aberrant radio-cast. He closed his eyes to think.

When he opened them his senses were suddenly struck by a clear blue sky and green everywhere. A cool breeze blew directly into his face stimulating the surface of his skin. His space suit was gone. All that remained was his form fitting clothing. He now sat on a tree stump in the middle of a field plush with life for as far as he could see. A multitude of insects danced from near to far giving the scene a feeling of constant movement.

He took a guarded breath then looked around frantically trying to gain his bearings. As he began to stand he was stopped by the voice.

"Isn't it wondrous?"

"Where am I? Who's there?" He continued looking about but could not locate its source. He tried to stand again, but found himself too weak to stay up. Slowly he fell back to the sitting position on the stump.

"Do you see it?" asked the voice. "Look, here it comes."

"See what?" Gray replied.

A flock of birds flew overhead and headed off into the distance.

"What's your name? And why can't I see you?"

"My name is Hezek. I am here."

In an instant a dark complexioned woman with a thin, athletic build stood in front of him. Smooth aquiline features were punctuated by piercing light brown eyes. She was slightly taller then he and also wore form fitting clothing. But the material in hers was bright silver and sparkled in the light of the sun.

"This place. Where am I?"

"This place," answered the woman "is my world, the world in which I was born."

Gray could hear what she was saying but noticed that her lips did not move.

"How am I hearing you?" he asked.

"I speak to your mind."

"My mind?"

"Your soul is maintaining it so that I may communicate with you."

"My soul?"

"That thing that will continue."

"I don't understand," said Gray. "What are you telling me?"

"You are about to move on, and, in the interim, we would like to give you knowledge about our past."

"Are you telling me that I'm here in spirit and you're talking to me in this spirit world…or something?" He looked around doubtfully. "If what you're telling me is true, then what good would this…knowledge do me anyway? And who are the 'we'?"

"We are as you."

Gray shook his head in disbelief.

"Even one's mental state during their last breath is of importance. The transition of experiences is seamless. Most are not aware of this in their consequent lives."

She mentioned his last breath. He realized, no matter what appeared to be happening now, or what sinister deception his weakening mind concocted in reality he did not have much time left.

"My mental state appears to be playing tricks on me," he said sarcastically.

"I am guiding this experience," she responded. "The mind is a powerful generator of physical delusions. In this case, the delusion is an accurate depiction of the past."

"But still a delusion," he returned cynically. "And if this place is supposed to be some alien planet and you're supposed to be some kind of alien, I hate to break the news to you, lady, but this looks an awful lot like earth and you sure do look like an African women. Or, judging from your knowledge of English, a woman from any town, USA."

"I think the message. You receive and interpret it. This is earth and I am what you in your time would call an African woman. This is the past."

"Forgive me and no pun intended, but unless the government has an alternative black-projects space program going on that you're a product of, then I'm going with the notion that I've just ran out of oxygen and I'm having a conversation with myself in my own head."

"Gray, thousands of years ago, I died like you are about to die."

Gray fell silent for a moment before responding.

"I'm listening."

"Our civilization was more advanced on every level then yours is now. The world was divided into two main groups. One group believed that technology was the answer to extending human survival. The much smaller group focused their energy entirely on the inner workings of the mind. Eventually the two went to war. It lasted for more them twenty five years."

"Twenty five years?" questioned Gray.

"The latter group were not like the psychics of your day for this was a concrete discipline and, when you are at war with yourself, it is difficult to distinguish who your opponent is."

"And who won this war?" Gray asked

"The first group," she answered, "which I was a part of."

Through the same mysterious link that was allowing him to hear what she was saying, Gray could sense a deep sadness emanate from Hezek.

"Sometimes," she said, "the only way to understanding is through death. I believe…we were wrong."

For the first time since his encounter with Hezek, Gray heard her hesitate which prompted him to explore this sensitive area while it was exposed. But, if this was all really happening, then she had already entered his mind. And, if she were already in his mind, then he speculated, she would know what he was about to do. He proceeded nonetheless.

"So if you won this war," he asked, "or even existed, how come Mr. Sterling in my high school history class never mentioned any of this?"

"Long before your recently recorded history there were three wars. The first was the 'alliance of the mind' versus technology. The second was for power over who would decide the direction of our technological advancements." She stopped.

"And the final war?" asked Gray.

"I died shortly after the Second World War, but have some knowledge of the events after my death."

"Some knowledge?" he questioned. "You seem to know a hell of a lot about everything else. Why the sudden forgetfulness?"

"It was a complicated time," she said, "and there are some things that are of no value to your present state of being."

"Try me," Gray responded. "Not that it makes a difference now anyway but, what the hell, maybe it'll take my mind off…"

It dawned on him that they had surely been there for longer than he had air left. Before he could mention it, Hezek addressed his thought.

"Time here," she said, "is moving more quickly then where your lower mind is located, for we are near the thin veil that separates the dream state from the subconscious.'

"I see," he responded knowingly. "So this is a dream."

"No. I am using the energy your mind would normally use to formulate dreams to portray the world you see before you."

"So I'm still out in space with little oxygen left…dreaming…And you're in my dreams?"

"When you closed your eyes," she responded, "I put you to sleep in order to use this state. I am only guiding your thoughts."

"OK," said Gray. "If that's so, then I've got nowhere else to be, so how about the rest of the story?"

"You really should experience it," said Hezek, and then disappeared.

For a couple of seconds Gray stared at the spot were she had been, expecting her to reappear. She did not.

The scene flickered. In an instant, all of the doubts and misgivings about what he was experiencing were gone. He suddenly found himself, not just witnessing all of the events Hezek had explained to him, but more.

It was midday, and he was moving above and about a battlefield where the fighters on both sides where obviously brothers of Hezek. One group was unarmed and greatly outnumbered. The other heavily equipped with mechanisms like he had never seen. The armed soldiers were rushing their unarmed brethren in waves…and dying in waves.

The scene jumped. Now he was beside one of the armed troopers and could feel fear and anxiety gripping the man's mind as he ran forward. Helplessly, Gray followed. The Trooper neared the front line and let out a screeching battle cry accompanied by a series of energy pulses emitted from his weapon. He took a couple of long strides before stopping abruptly. He fell to his knees in agony. Blood spurted from his ear and nasal openings. His eyes rolled up, then his head hit the ground.

A female soldier appeared. Keeping a low profile, she quickly removed items from her dead comrade, including his weapon. She was immediately up and running toward the battlefront, cutting right toward Gray. He looked directly at her. It was Hezek. He felt an urge to say something but knew it was useless. She continued toward the front line.

The scene changed again, and Gray found himself standing with the side that was unarmed. They were dressed in flowing, brightly colored clothing. He was positioned where assaults were taking place. He was surrounded by people of all ages, from children no more then a few years old, to the elderly. For a moment he thought he could hear a baby crying. Thoughts touched his awareness then faded away. Like the wind passing through a porous barrier, orders, ideas and commands entered Gray's mind, then were gone. Rapidly, he made sense of the situation. Their homes were nearby and this was a last stand. Amazingly, some of them held a barrier composed entirely of thought energy. Others met the onslaught of enemy fighters in a way that Gray had never dreamed possible. Each focused on a handful of soldier's heads or chests. Once a firm connection was made, an intense thought burst caused an aneurismal effect in their brains or hearts.

Again, the scene changed, unfolding into a night scene. From Hezek's story, Gray reasoned that he was now seeing the Second World War. Massive earthquakes followed intense blasts of light. Swift moving airships clashed above and below clouds of thick black smoke. Death came quickly to the unlucky ones, as the extreme weaponry expressed itself indiscriminately across the battlefield.

Suddenly, he was at the top of a small mountain range and a breathtaking vista. Below there were modern buildings spread out in a fertile land. The structures had simplicity but elegance in their designs. From Hezek's description there had been a third war but, from what he was seeing, he reasoned it must have taken place some time ago.

His reasoning was proved wrong.

A brilliant ball of light with an amber hue punctuated a new canvas. With a sizzling hum, the ball shot up and rose to a stop beneath a group of clouds. It held its position as if waiting. Gray's attention was completely captured by the orb. He was perplexed as to what he was seeing…until a few moments later when…

In rapid succession three more orbs, this time bright white in color, shot passed him making a whooshing sound. A second later, two more flew by. The first three had already made contact with the amber sphere and Gray observed them engage that sphere in a battle. The amber sphere was about to be overtaken by the five white orbs when second amber sphere appeared. Gray related the type of maneuvering he was seeing to a group of insects' erratic flight patterns when they cluster together in mid air. Little fingers of light appeared between them whenever an amber sphere came near a white sphere.

The two amber spheres periodically changed position, moving to an entirely different area of sky, causing the white spheres to follow. In rapid succession more fingers of light flashed between them. The next change in position brought them close. Low and in front of him they clashed, making turns and movements that he knew no craft occupied by a living being could make. They must be drones.

What were once the mysterious fingers of light shed their mystery, when suddenly one amber and one white sphere stopped a few meters away. They floated silently with a single beam connecting them. Because of its amber color, Gray deduced that the illuminated rod must be coming from the orb of the same distinction. Before the other white orbs were able to assist, the amber orb that was locked in with the white one shot away to another region of sky. The white sphere appeared to wobble in mid air, then dip down a couple of times before cracking open like an egg, partially revealing its contents before exploding into a large fireball.

More startling to Gray than their method of fighting or the explosion he had just witnessed was what he saw inside. It contained living occupants. He didn't know what they were he didn't but they were not human.

The amber craft returned to the fight and aggressively engaging the remaining ships. Gray could only imagine what the rest of the war was like.

Before his mind could even begin to hypothesize about what he had seen…

There was a beep.

The air was thick and difficult to inhale. He knew he was back…in space…with little oxygen left. His body ached all over as if he had been slammed back into it. All he could see were stars, everywhere. No earth, no moon, just stars for eternity. Panic gripped him for a moment as he glanced about frantically for something…anything familiar…an anchor to the life that he was about to leave behind. Suddenly through his mental haze a woman's voice sounded.

"Gray, is that you?"

"Julie," he answered back, gasping for air. "I…I understand."

"Gray, I'm so sorry." Her voice tapered off at the end as if it were difficult for her so speak.

"Julie, listen to me."

"Gray, it's OK, you don't have to say anything. Just close your eyes and we'll be here, with you, as long as we have to be."

"Close my eyes," he repeated. "No, please, I have to tell you something."

"Allright, I'm listening but..."

"I want you all to listen. This is wrong!"

"Gray, you don't have to..."

"We shouldn't be here! Not this way!"

"Gray, it's ok..."

"No it's not...Julie, listen to me." He hesitated as if gathering more energy. "We've chosen the wrong path. This is not the best way. We are not the first to be here and we won't be the last to make this...mistake." He took a labored breath. "Damn it, we need to understand ourselves before we can began to understand the world around us. I've seen so much...so much...history. Everything we've been taught about our distant past has been a lie."

"Gray, I don't know what you're..."

"Julie I've seen it for myself...I've experienced it. I understand what she was trying to tell me."

"She?" responded Julie.

"Hezek!" He shouted as if expecting an answer. "Now I know what she meant." He tried to continue but found it difficult to speak. The lack of oxygen was beginning to affect his ability to form coherent thoughts. The stars began to dim; his consciousness waned in and out, but before complete darkness overtook him, Gray managed to express one last thing to Julie...one last thing to all who were listening.

"Julie, the stars...the universe, are inside us...just...just...look deep...er..."

Everything around him narrowed, then faded. He knew he wanted to say more but was unable. He wanted to inhale just one last breath of life, but could not. As his hopes and dreams slid away behind him, so did his body from his soul.

Once again he felt the sensation of being slammed into something.

A radiant light appeared before him. The light grew quickly into the size of a large morning sun. He could hear voices in the distance, male, faintly at first then stronger. Gray thought he could decern what they were saying but soon realized he could not, because they were speaking...

...Russian. Two figures, silhouetted by the light, leaned over him. They began to tug and push at his limbs. He was now fully aware of being in his body which was in his space suit and aware of the two men standing over him. One of them moved away while the other hurriedly removed his helmet. It released with a snap letting a rush of warm air hit his face. The other man returned and spoke to Gray with a heavy accent.

"Mr. Braxton, welcome aboard our ship. There is someone who would like to talk with you." He slipped a head set on Gray while the one Russian turned his attention to removing his suit.

"Gray?" It was Julie.

"Julie," answered Gray with a groggy. "What happened?"

"There was an accident," she replied, "but you're OK now. A manned Russian orbiter was close enough to assist us."

"The Russians? How did they know what happened?"

"We asked them the same question. They couldn't guarantee they could get to you in time so I didn't want to give you false hope."

"The others?"

"I'm so very sorry," she said with sincere regret in her voice. "Just close your eyes and we'll take care of the rest."

Gray responded slowly. "Close my eyes?"

"Close your eyes," Julie said again.

"Yes…yes…I think I'll do that." Gray closed his eyes and slipped into a dream.

Chapter 9 of a Horror Story

The room fell silent. He straightened the sheets of paper he was holding and continued reading…

"Chapter 9"

Bursting from a group of trees his pounding heart kept cadence with each stride that he prayed would put a greater distance between him and his assailant. It was cold outside and had been dark for over an hour. As he made his way through an open field, streams of moonlight illuminated patches of frost that cracked beneath his feet. He forced his tall slender body to move as quickly as it could across the clearing to a broken down fence with trees just a few meters beyond. He slipped between an opening, stopped and looked back across the field. His eyes darted back and forth scanning the breadth of the dark open space. He saw nothing. The air from his fast, shallow breathing touched the chill of the night, creating a perpetual mist in front of his face.

To him, it didn't matter where he had been or where he was going. All that mattered was survival, just to stay alive long enough to try again. He desperately needed time to think, and to focus.

He looked up and down the length of the fence for some place to hide, when he noticed a structure; an old dilapidated house behind some trees a few hundred meters away. Before moving, he looked back once more. This time, his eyes caught sight of something.

Like the boogie man in a child's worst nightmare, or some frightening imaginary being that had suddenly come to life, a shadowy figure emerged at the other side of the clearing. His heart began to beat faster. Does it see me, he thought to himself.

It stopped. It would have completely blended in with its surroundings, but the light of the moon set off its husky body just enough for him to discern its silhouette. It stood at least three meters tall. Glowing blood-red pupils punctuated its large head. Its legs were thick like a Gorilla's, but longer. It had arms and hands like a human's, but they were joint-less like a snake and, from their size, more powerful.

How could he dream of something like this, he thought. So evil. He looked back at the house. I'm thinking too much…must conserve my mind's energy. He started running. The brisk air emboldened the beads of sweat that forced their way to the surface of his skin. They felt like thousands of tiny pinpricks as he rushed forward, knowing that the creature would be in pursuit.

So close now.

He was near enough to see that the door was hanging by one hinge -- an easy entry but little security.

Twin siblings of different parents, fear and terror, encircled his body. Fear driving him on. Terror stopping him from looking back to see if the monster was upon him.

He came to the door, hesitating long enough to pull it back so he could enter.

Aided by the light of the moon reaching in through a series of broken windows, he was able to identify a small empty room with a short hallway leading to the back. He moved quickly down it, into an even smaller room that had a tiny closet with another door that was open but still intact. He entered and shut himself inside. The space was pitch black, wreaked of rot, and so narrow he could barely move. He slid down into a fetal position and closed his eyes. Knowing there wasn't much time, he calmed himself and started clearing his mind.

Focus…Concentrate.

His consciousness became aware of three different worlds: The world of memories, of who he was and where he came from; the distinct world of horror that he now found himself in; and last, a world of impressions, the world where, he knew, the creator of the abomination around him resided. That was the place were his thoughts must be centered.

His mental energy narrowed.

Then…something connected.

"Please help me! I know that a man is reading a story in front of you at this moment. I can sense it. What he is saying now is not on the pages in front of him. But coming from me, whom all of you believe is a character in a story. Please someone help me! I don't have much time!

"My name is Kartma Relluf and I am a scientist from a universe that parallels yours. We thought we had found a way to move across life streams into your world but something went wrong. Terribly wrong. Your subconscious reality creates a vast barrier around my destination. And that is were I am trapped. This ether of thought is like a mine field of minds pulling energy into them and I've been caught over the mind of the man standing in front of you, periodically being drawn down into his stories. Our planet is dying…our fault. I may be our final hope.

"Believe me, please! I am a real living being speaking through him. I am not just a character lost in some chapter in a horror story! I can prove it. I sense that the room is large. The man who is interpreting my message is standing next to a desk. Off to his right is the person directing the class, a woman. She's leaning against an outside window. She is wearing a dark blue shirt and grey pants. By the outside door sits another woman with long black hair. Her shirt is white, her pants black. In the back corner of the room, there is a man with a brown shirt and blue pants. Please, anyone in this room, please rise and show me that you believe! I will feel the impression of your movement. If I could just connect with another mind, maybe I could find a way to escape. The man that I'm speaking through pulls so heavily from the subconscious that I am repeatedly sucked down a conduit into his creative thoughts.

"I believe my only hope is to move closer to someone else's mind, so please one of you stand up! Give me a sign that you're willing to try. Walk over to him so I can attempt to free myself from this hell that he has created.

"The being he has conjured…I can hear it outside. Please help me!

"This time, I think that the creator, the man who's standing in front of you, is going to kill me. I don't want to die like this!

"Oh my god! It's in the house. I can hear it moving down the hallway toward me. Please, someone please! It's on the other side of the door.

"If my people attempt to send another one of us, and they survive, give them this message.

"Tell my family that I love them."

Somewhere in Santa Barbara, California, the reader, a middle aged man stood next to an old desk in front of his writing class, staring at the pages of text he'd written the night before. He wasn't sure what he had just read, or if he had finished. He looked over at his instructor, a woman leaning against a window. She wore a short sleeved, blue shirt and light grey pants. By the outside door was another woman with long black hair, white shirt and black pants. He glanced to his left to see a balding older man wearing a brown top and blue pants. Not knowing what else to do, he scratched the back of his head and sat down in a nearby chair. He waited for questions and comments from the rest of the group.

"That was some story," said the instructor. "I'm not sure where it's going but I think it has potential. Let's see what the rest of the class has to say." She turned her attention to the other students who sat quietly until being prompted by her gaze.

Near the back of the room a young girl with short red hair slowly raised her hand. The instructor called on her. The girl spoke with apprehension.

"Was…that the end?"

The man shrugged his shoulders, answering slowly, "I don't know."

The class remained silent for a moment before the instructor called on the next reader.

That night a profound dream persuaded a writer somewhere in Southern, California, to leave the world of horror stories for the vast world of science fiction.

www.ingramcontent.com/pod-product-compliance
Lightning Source LLC
Chambersburg PA
CBHW051309170626
46809CB00004B/1821